MW01378139

CHALLENGING
Seasons

JOCEPHUS BINGHAM SR.

Copyright © 2024 Jocephus Bingham Sr.

All rights reserved. No part of this book may be reproduced, stored, or transmitted by any means—whether auditory, graphic, mechanical, or electronic—without written permission of both publisher and author, except in the case of brief excerpts used in critical articles and reviews. Unauthorized reproduction of any part of this work is illegal and is punishable by law.

ISBN: 979-8-89419-124-9 (sc)
ISBN: 979-8-89419-125-6 (hc)
ISBN: 979-8-89419-126-3 (e)

Because of the dynamic nature of the Internet, any web addresses or links contained in this book may have changed since publication and may no longer be valid. The views expressed in this work are solely those of the author and do not necessarily reflect the views of the publisher, and the publisher hereby disclaims any responsibility for them.

THE EWINGS
PUBLISHING

One Galleria Blvd., Suite 1900, Metairie, LA 70001
(504) 702-6708

Despite the chilly weather, winter offers ample opportunities for living and thriving. Regardless of who we are, the seasons impact everybody, and we must endure and adapt to this natural cycle. We must grasp and comprehend the different seasons and times we experience. So, enjoy the sun's rays and the smell of budding flowers. Life brings us happiness. But, it also has challenges like thunderstorms and winter.

INTRODUCTION

Life is, as usual, changing. Seasons mark it. Each season brings unique challenges and opportunities. Life has moments of enough and joy. It also has periods of adversity and struggle. These changing seasons shape our lives and assess our resilience. We must navigate personal hardships, societal upheavals, and global crises. Facing challenging times is an inevitable part of being human.

The Challenging Season Book shows us how to strengthen ourselves. The Saints must adapt to the changing tides and emerge transformed. In this exploration, we delve into tough seasons. We pray that everyone who reads this book will grasp their meaning. By following the steps of this book, we will learn the value of trusting Jesus. Everybody will find the hidden potential for growth and renewal it offers.

The Challenging Season Book is unique. It explores the ebbs and flows of life. It offers guidance on how to navigate the challenges we face. The book acknowledges that life has many seasons. Each has its own set of trials and triumphs. The narrative sets the stage for readers to accept change and adversity as chances for growth and change.

Challenging Seasons emphasizes the importance of resilience in adversity. It highlights that tough times are inevitable. But they also bring opportunities for personal growth and renewal. The book encourages readers to delve into tough times. It aims to help them find hidden lessons and growth potential. The author's prayer is by reading this book. The individual will gain the power to become stronger and experience a transformative change.

His statement aligns with the Bible (1 Peter 1:18-21) that life is a journey of hardships and joy. People can build resilience by embracing and learning from all experiences. They can also find more intellectual meaning.

The Challenging Season Book offers a full view of navigating life's difficulties. It gives valuable insights and tools for readers to grow and thrive in demanding times.

CHAPTER 1

"For everything, there is a season and a time for every purpose under heaven." — Ecclesiastes 3:1

The Challenging Seasons

The world shifts from one demanding situation to the next. People worry about the outcome of new events, which causes fear. Yet, fearfulness causes us to miss many excellent opportunities. It is ordinary to be afraid. When we become discouraged by the unknown, as is appropriate and natural, Christians should continue their journey, regardless. Every problem has a physical and spiritual solution.

The Psalmist writes, "Our flesh and heart may fail, but GOD is our heart's strength and portion forever." Psalm 73:26.

Helen Keller wrote: "Avoiding danger is no safer in the long run than outright exposure. As often as the bold catch the fearful."

Helen's message highlights life's risks and challenges. Regardless, we must be cautious in some situations. However, being too cautious does not guarantee complete safety or success. Some risks may be necessary for personal growth, learning, and achieving goals.

The act of balancing caution and openness has the potential to yield greater rewards and chances. It motivates people to leave their comfort zones when suitable. It is challenging to move from our happy place. Save for planned risks can bring valuable results.

For instance, Emily is a Christian working out at the same gym as Doctor Bingham. She shared with him how she was content with her life. She had a routine that she followed and was comfortable with the familiarity. But deep down, a spark flickered within her. It was a desire for something more, something beyond her comfort zone.

One Sunday morning, a poster caught her eye as Emily walked past the Church's bulletin board. It advertised a mission trip overseas to dig wells and build a worship school center. The mere thought made Emily's heart flutter with joy. She was eager to embark on the adventure. Yet, she tells how her mind loves comfort. So, she hesitated, clinging to her routine safety.

Fate would have it that Emily's friend Thomas ran into her. He found her standing before the poster, lost in thought. Thomas was a Spirit-filled soul, always seeking challenging experiences to do good. Sensing Emily's hesitation, he nudged her, speaking, "Why not step out of your comfort zone, Emily? Imagine the testimonies we could tell if we ventured into this overseas village!"

Emily shared how she experienced a surge of fear and excitement coursing through her veins. So, Thomas encouraged her. He stirred her righteous Spirit. The hesitant young lady changed her life forever. She signed up for the trip, determined to leave her comfort zone behind and embrace the unknown.

Still scared stiff, she arrived on the day of the mission trip after hours of travel. Emily stood at the edge of the village with a group of fellow missionaries. The next day, they delved deep into the work. Thus, the work had challenges and obstacles they had never imagined. But with each hurdle, they overcame. Emily had a rush of exhilaration in her veins. It excited her to talk about the hidden treasures of sharing

Jesus. She spoke of seeing people who had never worshipped Christ come to know Him. The once frightened girl explained she forged bonds with her companions that would last a lifetime.

Through their journey's trials, Emily learned something. "True growth lies outside one's comfort zone." So, as we cry happy tiers, she discovers the courage she never knew she had. It unlocked a world of dreams. The once-petrified lady emerged from the village with a new purpose. The mission trip filled her heart with gratitude and courage for the adventure that had changed her life.

From that day forward, Emily vowed never to let fear hold her back. She knew she could only embrace life's journey by stepping out of her comfort zone. Emily set forth with an open heart and a fearless Spirit each day. She was ready to explore the wonders that awaited her beyond a fearful horizon.

Trust Jesus

Further, the burdens of existence can become overwhelming. So, when faced with challenges, we might question if we should seek strength from Christ. Our encounters and obstacles may appear overwhelming, yet they are conquerable. Setbacks throw us off GOD's intended path. But they can lead us to ultimate achievements, satisfaction, and joy.

Still, none of our problems can occur without GOD's permission. But He uses everything that happens to His children for good, even when others mean it for evil. (Romans 8:28).

This book (The Challenging Seasons) offers both inspiration and motivation to keep going. It also has practical steps. It helps you overcome tough times and become the person you aspire to be. That person survives and thrives. The title suggests that by trusting Jesus Christ. We can navigate the challenges of different life seasons.

But unfounded fear will cause us to risk stagnating and staying stuck in a rut. However, spiritual struggles can make us see problems as chances for personal and group growth. For example, difficulties let Christ's supporters use their resilience and creativity to navigate challenging times. The Apostle Paul writes, "Our troubles are light and brief. They bring an eternal glory that far outweighs them all." 2 Corinthians 4:17-18.

So, seeking support from the Almighty empowers Christians. Adaptability through Christ and a positive outlook help us beat fear. Alarming emotions allow us to embrace opportunities. Fear is natural. However, Christians can rely on faith in Jesus and a positive outlook. They use these to face fearful challenges, coupled with resilience and hope. Support, flexibility, and Bible teachings are the foundation. We use them to conquer fear and embrace opportunities.

But Christian apprehensions cause hesitation. It can stop the Saints from seizing opportunities. Yet, facing troubles through Jesus, fear can pave the way for new experiences, learning, and personal growth. We must acknowledge something. Growth often comes when individuals face and surpass their worries. So, as we develop a mindset that embraces challenges, chances for growth are beneficial. Besides, The LORD tells us:

"You have nothing to fear, as I am by your side to offer my unwavering support." Isaiah 41:10.

Yet, any fearful challenge the Saint faces will be nothing new, according to (Ecclesiastes 1:9). King Solomon drafted this unique Devotional Book. Please understand it is ordinary to encounter challenges, but they are manageable. He encourages people to face them with resilience. Jesus (the Blessed and Only Ruler) tells us to have peace in Him since the world can only offer tribulation. So, He urges us to take heart because He has overcome the world." Thus, we will defeat struggles when we trust what the Almighty can do.

"Both riches and honor come from You; You rule overall. In Your Hand are power and might; within Your Hand, it is to make great and give strength to all." 1 Chronicle 29:12.

In the above Scripture, the writer encourages the Saints to find peace in faith. They should do this despite difficulties and tribulations. The belief is that by faith in Jesus. Individuals can find the strength to beat challenges. Jesus (THE AUTHOR of LIFE, Acts 3:15) has triumphed over the world.

Apostle John quotes Him: "In the world, you will have tribulation, but be of good cheer; I have overcome the world" (John 16:33).

The beloved writer tells the Glorified that they can conquer their fears. They can do it by embracing the troubling prospects in Christ's Name that might hold them back. GOD is faithful. He will not let His people suffer more than they can manage.

For instance, The LORD assures His followers will not face trials or temptations. They will be the ones they can control. He will give a way out or strength to endure. Then, He will be the source of comfort and strength during challenging times. When facing encounters or adversity, rely on your faith and beliefs. Together, they will give you solace, inspiration, and purpose.

In the prophet's book, Chapter 41, verse 10, the forecaster Isaiah writes: "Fear not, for The LORD is with us. Be not dismayed, for I am your Jehovah Jireh. I will strengthen, help, and hold you up with my right hand." Then, in Chapter 46, verses 1-3, the Psalmist writes, "GOD (Jesus) is our protection and strength. He is always available to help us in trouble." These Verses say believers can find strength and refuge in the Almighty. It is true even when they face overwhelming challenges. It encourages trust in GOD's presence and protection during tough times.

As we face fear, we build strength, courage, and confidence. "There is no need to be afraid because I am here with you." "He who is not courageous enough to take risks will accomplish nothing in life." We may face multiple setbacks, but we must never allow ourselves to be defeated.

CHAPTER 2

The future holds many more significant opportunities and experiences than anything we leave behind on our journey.

Challenges Persist

Scientists and academic institutions have studied global issues in recent decades. They try to analyze all the events that cause problems. They assess the threats, reduce them, and show us steps to solve them. Brilliant minds from all nations have analyzed issues from different angles and perspectives.

Even politicians use critical thinking skills to check catastrophes and identify potential solutions. Sometimes, they try different approaches to see what works. They prepare to adapt based on the outcomes.

Regardless, predicaments yet exist. Natural and human-made tragedies still happen despite humankind's efforts, local and worldwide. These events have devastated individuals, communities, and entire regions. Mitigating and responding to such catastrophes is an enormous challenge. It is a challenge on a large scale. Tacticians face these challenges. Countries invest billions in disaster preparation. Hence, they build a robust infrastructure. Nations also foster community engagement and education.

Yet, global challenges, including deadly diseases, persist. Inclusive are economic instability, political and social disorder, and natural calamities.

For example, our metropolis is bustling. We have skyscrapers reaching for the heavens. Our streets are alive with energy. Yet amid them is an adverse tapestry woven in humanity's threads. Each thread represents a unique part of the globe and a distinctive culture. They have distinct identities, but we are all interconnected. Bound by the commonality of existing on this fragile planet.

That said, whispers of concern interrupt the ceaseless rhythm of urban life. They echoed through the countryside, alleys, and avenues. People once saw the world as boundless in terms of resources and possibilities. But now, we stand at a crossroads. Humankind faces challenges that cross borders and defy standard solutions.

Climate change leads to these challenges. It is an existential threat that looms over all humanity. For example, the ice caps are melting. The signs of ecological imbalance are clear. They are in the Arctic and the scorched equatorial lands. Seas are rising and encroaching on coastal cities. Wildfires ravage vast forests. Erratic weather hurt farming, threatening food security for millions.

In response to this global crisis, voices worldwide have risen in unison. They advocate urgent action and cooperation regarding these challenges. Leaders convened summits and conferences. They pledged to cut carbon emissions, switch to renewable energy, and save biodiversity. Yet, amid the grand declarations and lofty promises, skepticism lingered. Vested interests and bureaucracy fueled it with inertia.

Meanwhile, in the corridors of power, geopolitical tensions simmered. They cast a shadow over international cooperation. Old rivalries and new conflicts threatened to derail efforts to address shared challenges. Nations jostle for dominance in a more connected world. Still, the fear of nuclear proliferation, regional conflicts, and asymmetric warfare haunt humanity. It reminds us of peace's fragility in a discord-filled world.

Yet, amidst the turmoil and uncertainty, there are glimmers of hope. They come from the resilience and ingenuity of the Christian faith. But the Saints must continue to come together to show righteous solutions. Christian Holiness harnessed the power of grassroots activism coupled with free enterprise. So, we can use the Bible as a spiritual toolbox to tackle the world's issues. The issues include poverty, inequality, healthcare, and education access.

For example, in far-off places, indigenous righteous peoples stood as custodians of ancient wisdom. They preserved Holy traditional knowledge and practices. These offered insights into living in harmony with nature. But society marginalizes and overlooks Christian voices. Still, Christianity carried the wisdom of generations. Thus, Holiness serves as a reminder of the interconnectedness of all life on earth.

So, the good news is this: humanity continued to change. Each thread of human culture intertwines with others. We make a diverse and resilient mosaic. The world faced daunting challenges. Nonetheless, Christians are a catalyst for transformation. Christianity's actions serve as an inspiration for all people. It inspires nations to rise above hardship. Holiness also encourages them to strive for a fair, lasting future.

Righteous Holiness is on the horizon. Thus, sacredness casts a golden glow on the humanity underneath. The threads of Christianity remain intertwined. They wove a story of perseverance, compassion, and collective effort. Faced with global challenges, the strength of any one thread did not matter. What mattered was the resilience and sanctification of the Church, which Jesus built on the imperishable rock. (Matthew 16:18).

Further, Christianity has shown remarkable resilience throughout its history, enduring persecutions, schisms, and challenges. Sainthood has faced suppression and opposition. But it has persisted and adapted for over two thousand years. The bedspread of righteousness has spread across diverse cultures and regions. Yet the Holy Scriptures are indestructible and inerrant because GOD breathed them (2 Timothy 3:16–17; John 17:17).

Hence, Christian theology has proven resilient. Therefore, an unchallengeable conviction can address and adapt to changing ideas, cultures, and societies. Again, core beliefs of righteousness are constant. However, interpretations and applications of doctrine have changed. But they changed to meet the needs and challenges of different dispensations.

Christianity has shown resilience. It can blend with and change many cultures worldwide. For example, sainthood absorbed local traditions, practices, and beliefs. Righteousness adds to culture's broad appeal and adaptability.

The Christian Bible and its parishioners have shown resilience in tough times. They offer support, comfort, and solidarity with their members during challenging seasons. These include persecution, natural disasters, and social upheaval.

However, Christianity remains the world's most immense faith. Yet, secularism is rising. Christian affiliation is falling in some regions. Still, it has a significant presence on every continent. Its resilience is apparent. Holiness continues to grow, especially in areas like Africa and Asia.

The resilience of Christianity has many sides. It includes historical, doctrinal, cultural, communal, and global aspects. These show its lasting power and ability to change.

CHAPTER 3

While sickness can be unpleasant, it can also lead to unfamiliar experiences or personal advancement.

GOD Heals The Toughest Challenges

St. Louis, Missouri, is a bustling city. It nestles between the towering Gateway Arch, busy streets, and the Mississippi River. A young man named Robert lived there. Robert's life was always full of laughter and joy until a dark cloud appeared one day.

It started with a routine visit to the doctor's office. Robert had been feeling unwell for weeks. But despite that, the news he received shook him to his core: he had a rare and aggressive cancer. His world seemed to crumble around him, and fear gripped his heart like never.

As Robert began treatment, he battled not only pain but also doubts and fears. The agony threatened to consume him. Yet, amidst the darkness, a glimmer of hope remained—his unwavering faith in Jesus Christ.

Every day, Robert would turn to his Bible for strength and solace. Further, he prayed without stopping. The unhealthy man showed formidable feelings and trusted that The LORD would guide him through the storm. He clung to the promise in (Hebrews 13:5). GOD promised not to leave him — despite the uncertainty of life.

So, each day, Robert's faith grew. He saw glimpses of light piercing the darkness. His friends and family loved and supported him. This encouragement gave him moral strength and determination. He faced each challenge.

Still, often, the pain seemed unbearable. Doubts threatened to overwhelm him. But in those moments, Robert would hear from The Wiser: "You can do all things through Me who gives you strength."

Countless prayers and his medical team's expertise helped. Robert's condition improved. He regained his strength, and the cancer retreated. It was a long and arduous journey, but Robert refused to lose hope.

At last, after months of treatment and countless prayers, Robert got the news he had been longing to hear. He was cancer-free. Tears of joy streamed down his face like a gentle waterfall as he thanked GOD for His faithfulness and mercy.

As Robert emerged from the darkness, he knew his journey was not about beating cancer. It was about finding the depth of his faith in Jesus Christ. He had learned to rely on Him more than ever through trials and tribulations. In Jesus, The Hope of Glory King Eternal (1 Timothy 1:17). Robert had found the strength to overcome.

Today, Robert's life is a testament to the power of faith. It shows the incredible miracles that happen when we trust in Jesus. Storms may rage, and challenges seem insurmountable. But, with GOD by our side, we can overcome anything in His Name.

Also, people can face hardships. These include spontaneous abuse, addiction, discrimination, homelessness, and political unrest. That said, millions of Christians face unprecedented hardship. They come from past and present troubles. The above remonstrances could cause traumatic experiences that affect long-term well-being.

Then, it seems every believer reminds us to have unwavering faith. And to place our trust in GOD. Yet, in certain situations, that is easier said than done. It will be easier if we oversee it ourselves. Nobody ever said having faith would be easy, but it will be worth it.

GOD knows everything we are going through. He knows how to oversee every situation to get the best outcome. We need to follow his path and trust that he understands. But when you ask, you must believe. Do not doubt! Doubters are like sea waves. The wind blows and tosses them."—James 1:6.

Twelve Hopeless Years

"A travel-sick lady in the Bible was hemorrhaging for twelve long years. She had sought medical help and spent all her money on doctors. But none could cure her." Luke 8:43-48.

Luke, one author of the New Testament, provides an account of a significant event. A woman suffered from bleeding for twelve years. But her faith in Jesus healed her. Her story emphasizes the power of belief and the compassion of Jesus towards those who seek him for help.

This Passage is from the Gospel of Matthew 9:20–22, Mark 5:24b–34, and Luke 8:42b–48. It shows the profound importance of faith and the kind nature of Jesus. She endured for many years and spent all her money seeking medical help. Yet, her faith leads her to believe that touching the edge of Jesus' clothes could heal her.

Jesus acknowledges her faith and commends her for it. The LORD heals her: "Daughter, your faith has made you well; go in peace." This story underscores the importance of faith in experiencing spiritual and physical healing. It shows Jesus will help those who seek Him. When we come to Christ, The Father will forgive our sins with faith and sincerity. He will also prepare us to return to Him.

That said, it is common for many Christians to stop their spiritual growth too soon. Obstacles result in energy exhaustion. Then, they become complacent. The person struggling with difficulties must get a little past their problem. But this is hard for several reasons:

(1) Somebody hurt them
(2) The commitment failed
(3) Because of unforeseen events, their life plans stalled

And so, how many faithful Christians would have wanted to be closer to Christ? But circumstances stopped them from returning. Many Jesus supporters stray from their commitment to Him. It happens because of life's interference and the rise of obstacles.

Yet, faithful Christians do not see themselves as citizens of this world. We see in Philippians 3:20 that our rightful citizenship is in heaven. The Saints are in the world and face temptation, suffering, and trials. But the faithful must not live and respond as the world does. We renounce the ways of the world and pledge our loyalty to Jesus and His Kingdom.

So, the Christian goal is to attain salvation in heaven. However, there are always obstacles. Whenever we lay the groundwork for our goals, problems will come to distract us. Plans seem so right, but then other things get in the way. The complicated answer is life and obstructions. Still, GOD wants us to work our way through problems.

For instance, what difficulties must the hemorrhaging woman overcome to reach Jesus? Two struggles:

(1) They deem the woman unclean according to cultural beliefs. Blood is coming from her. Many ancient laws in the Old Testament forbade associating with unclean people. Here is an example from Leviticus 15:19, 25-27; please read. The Scriptures show Leviticus says this woman's bleeding is unclean and untouchable.

For example, a woman's period impurity lasts seven days. Anyone who touches her is unclean until evening. However, she seems to have had a menstruating issue for twelve years. The Law required her to stay secluded. She could touch nothing, fearing giving her uncleanliness to others. Also, anything she rests on while menstruating becomes impure. The same goes for anywhere she sits.

Likewise, theologians have said that GOD chose certain things as unclean (see Genesis Chapter 7). He did so for His people's health. Hence, in Jesus' day, Jews were not to cook pork to avoid getting sick. Nonetheless, diseases can spread through body fluids. The Bible had it right about how infectious diseases spread even back then.

But the menstruating woman was frantic and anxious, as if this was her last desperate effort. Being unclean, she would face disapproval of being in a large crowd in this society. Yet, on she came! She was tenacious and would not stop trying until she accomplished her goal.

Everybody avoided unclean women. They did so as they went about their day. People would avoid brushing, touching, or sharing gestures on the path with her. She lived in isolation and had a reputation for being unclean. Doubtless, she is living in inaccessibility.

However, loneliness can affect the body, mirroring the physiological responses to physical pain. "Emotional distress, over time, can trigger a cascade of hormonal and neurological reactions. These cause chronic inflammation and weaken the immune system."

Thus, social isolation can cause anxiety, depression, and low self-esteem in individuals. But her faithful tenacity wanted to touch The LORD's garment for healing. So, she displayed a none-quit effort until she reached her goal.

A note: women understand bleeding. They have a monthly cleansing process. Each month, they endure a challenging time of body loss. Blood outside the body has long been unclean, even in Biblical times.

Once again, the bleeding, single-minded woman showed courage, persistence, and competence. Every Saint should take a lesson from her. But the most crucial question now is:

(2) What does life look like when looking back at the problems?

In hindsight, life's many issues seem huge. But we overcame temporary hurdles. With time, we see that what seemed like a significant setback was a steppingstone. It was a path to personal growth, resilience, or even more excellent opportunities.

Therefore, despite the lady's sickness and uncleanliness, the woman reached Jesus. Instead of condemning this female for her polluted touch, He cleansed and made her whole. So, we must ask another question!

In society's eyes, what makes us undeserving? Could it be how we see ourselves? Was it that crazy thing we did as teenagers? Or is it our societal standing? Still, whether earned, a reputation can be hard to shake. However, how we view ourselves can play a big part in our actions and interactions with others.

Besides, ethnicity, location, or meeting group expectations does not influence success. Here is the thing about Jesus. Many people give up because they want society to change so they can conform. But Jesus says, no, come, and I will change you from the inside outside. But if we wait for the community to change so we will fit it, we will stagnate in our faith. From then on, Jesus spoke, "Turn to GOD and change how you think and act because the kingdom of heaven is near!" Matthew 4:17.

Let us inspect this menstruating woman's faith more closely. An enormous crowd is pressing upon Jesus: "As Jesus was on His way, the crowds almost crushing Him" (Luke 8:42). The journey to reach Jesus would have been a formidable challenge for anyone. But it is ultra-challenging for her because of her medical condition.

Besides, they allowed Jairus, the synagogue ruler, to access the Savior. Yet, they would not have taken such action for someone of lower stature.

Contrariwise to, we go unnoticed by everyone as an unhealthy nobody. Regardless, do you perceive yourself as insignificant? Deuteronomy 28:13 emphasizes, "GOD will make us the head, not the tail." Also, the Saints' faith stops progressing when they allow what people say or think to come between them and Jesus. The Christian journey might pose a significant stumbling block ahead of us. But The LORD is aware of our identity and awaits our arrival.

Achievement gives us a sense of accomplishment. We could ask this menstruating woman. She would tell us that nothing beats the feeling of conquering. Her journey once seemed impossible. Yet, overcoming obstacles motivated her and reminded her she could do anything focused on Jesus. She accomplished her mission!

Though the crowd was pressing in on Christ from all sides, He sought: "Who touched me?" (Luke 8:45).

To recapitulate, the woman had to exhibit fragility to get close to the Savior. In lay terms, she had to navigate through the crowd to reach Jesus. And her prowess has not gone un-noted. It was a challenge. Nonetheless, this woman suffered from a long-lasting ailment that weakened her physical strength.

However, the unwell woman moved with stealth grace as she tried to fade into the background. Even though she was still sick, she maneuvered through the dense crowd to reach Jesus. She made sure her actions went unnoticed. The bizarre lady experienced instant healing when she touched The LORD's garment. She wanted to go undetected.

But the Savior had more incredible plans in store for her! Jesus refused to let her go unseen in the crowd. It surprised His disciples when Jesus stopped and asked who touched Him. (Luke 8:45).

They all denied it. But Peter highlights the Master, "The people are crowding and pushing against You!" Is it not strange that we try to devise a secular answer for the supernatural? But Jesus focuses attention on, "Someone touched Me. The power goes out of Me." Jesus turned and saw her. "Take heart, daughter; your faith has healed you." At that moment, the woman's healing takes place.

The woman needed a spiritual transformation. But let us go beyond the healing. Jesus' words, "Your faith has healed you, go in peace," are essential. Healing and peace are miracles! It is where every Christian must go beyond their problems!

"Do not fear, for I am with you, and do not worry, for I am your GOD. I will strengthen, help, and uphold you with my righteous right hand." GOD promises to offer comfort to those who seek Him. Remember this comforting Bible verse when pain and illness hit you or your loved ones? Isaiah 41:10.

CHAPTER 4

Christians have, throughout history, recognized the importance of infrastructure development. Today, addressing infrastructure challenges aligns with our commitment to life, well-being, and the common good.

Christianity Infrastructure Built To Meet Challenges

Infrastructure's significance

Christian infrastructure is crucial for Christian development, social progress, environmental sustainability, and resilience to the world's challenges. The Saints who invest in Holy concepts know it is essential for building prosperous, inclusive, resilient societies.

What makes Christian infrastructure crucial? For instance, consider the connection between spiritual matters and their natural counterparts. In 1 Corinthians 15:46, the Bible says that the natural came before the spiritual. The connection between them is powerful, making it impossible to break.

For instance, humankind relies on visuals to comprehend spiritual concepts. Thus, The LORD spent millennia developing pictures for man to grasp His salvation. For example, people needed millions of animal sacrifices to learn about the challenging cost of transgressions. Also, the Law was necessary for them to understand Jehovah's ways. And GOD required a Temple so humankind could know His presence. Centuries of detailed prophecies, they foretold the coming of the Messiah.

The Supreme Being came to this planet as Jesus. After centuries of preparation, the Messiah manifested Himself as the invisible Infinite Spirit. GOD's nature is now precise to all. He is Jesus! His Holy Nature represents love, light, and truth to meet humanity's challenges. All genders can now understand, believe, and ask the Almighty to forgive their sins.

So, the "Christian infrastructure" refers to the framework and structures supporting Christian faith activities. Here are the key components:

1. Places of Worship where Christians gather for worship, prayer, and Holy ceremonies.
2. Christian denominations have structures overseeing local congregations and regions.
3. Christian schools, colleges, and universities offer education from a Christian viewpoint.
4. Missionary Organizations spread the Christian faith through evangelism, aid, and development.
5. Christian infrastructure includes media outlets, publishing houses, and online platforms. They share Christ-centered teachings, literature, music, and other Christian media.
6. Many Christian Churches and ministries offer social services. It provides support for food, healthcare, housing, and disaster relief. They offer aid both nationally and internationally.

7. Christian denominations have ordained pastors, priests, ministers, and bishops. They offer spiritual guidance and oversee faith life in congregations.
8. Financial Infrastructure encompasses Christian organizations' fundraising, tithing, and financial resource management. It involves budgets, accounting systems, and fundraising campaigns.

The Christian infrastructure supports Christian activities globally. It includes institutions, organizations, and individuals. Holy networks serve the world's challenges through Biblical purposes.

That being so, Christians had much to do with shaping the world to withstand trials. They built a support system. Exemplar Christian communities founded early educational institutions, valuing knowledge and education. These institutions have shaped societies' intellect and culture. Faithful believers strengthened them against challenges.

These faith-based ministry constructions continued to stand tall. They are a symbol of faith and resilience in an ever-changing world. The Local Church relies on stone and wood for its infrastructure buildings. But also, its proper spiritual structure lay in the hearts of those who called it home. Thus, the Christian faith comes together in their belief in the power of love and the promise of redemption.

Regardless of trials, persisting. Christianity provides a robust support system for individuals going through tough times. So, the Glorified community's shared beliefs and the teachings of resilience are fundamental. Thus, the teachings of Christ play a significant role in humanity. Righteousness helps the Saints withstand trials. Believers in Jesus will draw strength from their faith. They will find comfort in the infrastructure of prayer and fellowship. Besides, they must trust in His higher purpose or Divine plan.

Also, many faith-based communities offer resources. These include counseling, shelters, rehab programs, and outreach. They help people in challenging situations. GOD gives us the responsibility to seek medical treatment and to pray for healing. Besides, Jesus acknowledged the necessity of doctors for individuals who were sick. "It is not the healthy who needs a doctor, but the sick." (Matthew 9:12). So, get medical help. Yet, it is vital to seek GOD's aid foremost.

Still, this may sound strange. But the Christian Bible teaches that even dreadful things help believers. For example, "We know all things work for the good of those who love GOD. The Son calls us according to his purpose." (Romans 8:28).

Spiritual Infrastructure

Because of sin, spiritual infrastructure is crucial for Christians to thrive in the modern world. We should allocate resources to construct, maintain, and overhaul our spiritual substructure, much like we do for physical and human infrastructure. It includes dedicating time to practices like spiritual reading, devotions, and receiving sacraments.

For example, in Ephesians, Chapter Six, the Apostle Paul describes the basic (infrastructure) armor of GOD. Paul skillfully examined the attire of a Roman soldier. He likens it to the clothing Christians need in their battle against evil.

Likewise, Ephesians Chapter Six resonates with our struggle to follow GOD's teachings. Life is a battle of the spirits. Paul's advice: "Be strong in The LORD and His power." His Book is one of the great realities of life. The Apostle shows how the world is deceiving. Humanity has more going on than what meets the eye. For example, behind the scenes, spiritual rulers are orchestrating global movements.

So, the Words in this Passage suggest the ongoing battle to live according to GOD's path. We fight the battle of life on a spiritual level. So, consider his words: "In conclusion, my fellow believers, find strength in The LORD and His mighty power." Equip yourself with the complete infrastructure of GOD to resist the devil's cunning. We are not fighting against flesh and blood but against spiritual powers and authorities of darkness. (Ephesians 6:10-13).

In lay terms, Paul acknowledges our vulnerability to Satan and his demonic powers. Therefore, Christians should recognize this, even if world leaders do not. So, intelligent planning is crucial for spiritual success. It is vital for our well-being. The Saints can overlook this reality and perceive carefree living. But we are in a perpetual fight against spiritual forces. However, Jehovah provides us with the spiritual infrastructure for warfare.

So, the spiritual armor GOD gives us is essential for Christian protection. Each defense mail piece serves as a robust framework for a specific purpose. They shield us from unseen spiritual attacks. Trusting in GOD and wearing His support armature, we stand firm against the enemy and draw closer to The LORD.

Thus, the infrastructure armament of GOD is essential for navigating through the world's problems. For instance, the temptations disguise the devil's deception. GOD warns us to resist the evil spirit's temptation in Ephesians 6:12. So, we must wear the protective clothing GOD has given us. The coat of mail has a unique structure to protect us from spiritual warfare, the attacks we cannot see altogether with our own eyes. Yet, with the formidable defenses, we can stand firm against the enemy and get closer to the Supreme Being.

GOD's mighty infrastructure suit of mail comprises a belt, chest plate, shoes, shield, helmet, and sword. Each piece has a significant meaning. For example, the belt stands for truth. As we wear the belt of truth, it safeguards us from the enemy's attempts to deceive us with lies. Stay truthful and fight off any lies or deceit. The chest plate signifies righteousness, protecting our hearts and trust in GOD. The shoes represent the Gospel's message of peace, encouraging us to remain positive.

Paul examined the Christian armor infrastructure with precision. The Christian protective clothing defends but can also protect as an offensive weapon. Any weakness or chink in one's coat of mail can lead to vulnerability. If one piece of armament is missing or damaged, we will compromise our spiritual safety. Ephesians Chapter Six emphasizes wearing the 'whole armor of GOD' twice. Incomplete armor makes us vulnerable to spiritual attack. It is not our coat of mail, but 'GOD's protective clothing.' Regular fellowship with the Holy Spirit and reading GOD's Word helps us wear His formidable defenses.

CHAPTER 5

It is crucial to remember not to consider guilt when deciding to begin anew.

A New Life Brings New Challenges

It is often exciting and scary after we embrace a new phase of life. It could start a new job, move to a different city, begin a relationship, or make any other meaningful change. But each new chapter brings challenges and chances for growth. Below are strategies to navigate these difficulties:

Approach new disputes with an open mind. Be adaptable. Then, you can navigate life's uncertainties with confidence and grace. Each new experience offers a chance to grow and discover. They will enrich your journey and shape your future. So, Christians should welcome the challenge of meeting new people.

For example, St. Louis's Central West End is charming. The building nestles among the Fox Theater, St. Louis, and Washington University. It also has some of the most fantastic restaurants in the United States. It held the Glad Tidings Word Fellowship Missionary Baptist Church. The building, weathered by time, yet full of whispers of faith.

The parishioners of Glad Tidings knew every stone of its walls and every echo of its corridors. Yet, a gentle breeze carried the promise of change on a tranquil Sunday morning. Despite the many sermons, the congregation was hostile and antagonistic toward meeting new people.

However, a stranger sat as an unfamiliar figure in the pew one Sunday morning. The man's presence is like a lone star in a darkened sky. He introduced himself to Doctor Bingham. Christopher's face had a mysterious glow. His eyes were pools of deep thought. They scanned the ancient walls and ceiling as if he sought comfort in their embrace.

In the bustling part of the city, the Church stood. However, they seldom opened their doors to strangers and kept their hearts shut. The members of Glad Tidings were friendly folk among themselves. But they kept to themselves and shunned outsiders. The Church services began and ended within its four walls.

Rumors whispered through the community. A recluse man named Mr. Grimsby was the head deacon who inhabited the congregation. He took pleasure in insulting parishioners. So, no one dared approach him, fearing the chilling glare that accompanied any intrusion.

Nonetheless, despite being independent, the worshippers of Glad Tidings lived in harmony. But they lived within their secluded world. They exchanged quick nods in passing. Except the conversations were rare. Children played in the yard. Yet, the somber atmosphere enveloping the congregation muffled their laughter.

Still, Christopher visits the Church. Despite the coldness, he considered this to be where GOD called him to serve. The stranger attempted to befriend the members with wide-eyed innocence, offering warm smiles. Despite his efforts, he faced hostility. The parishioners had no interest in welcoming outsiders into their secluded midst.

They gave him the cold shoulder. But Christopher persisted. The young man was persistent in overcoming their apathy. He bought flowers from a Schnucks supermarket. He gave them to widows and single mothers. Besides that, he spent time with their children. The young stranger had group prayer with the men. Mr. Grimsby was inclusive.

A subtle change occurred in Glad Tidings Church as weeks turned into months. The once-empty pews now boasted caring parishioners. A soft scent of Holiness tinged the air. The frosty congregation thawed. Resolute smiles and tentative greetings replaced the stiff demeanor.

Then Mr. Grimsby's stern face and attitude softened. He saw Christopher tending to his neglected garden. With a gruff voice that belied a hint of gratitude, he thanked him for bringing a spark of life back to Glad Tidings. From that day on, the Church members opened their doors and hearts to strangers. Visitors realized that kindness could flourish even in unsympathetic places.

So, the once cold congregation is now cordial and compassionate. The members are a testament to the power of Holy friendship.

Thus, amid the wind's whispers and the Church's silence in Glad Tidings, the story of the new individual in Christ echoed. It was a testament to the lasting power of love, grace, and the unwavering light that guides us home. So, GOD can use any method or means to make a new person out of them. The best feeling in the world is turning the page.

A note: our experiences are not of our own making; others, on average, shape them. On this twisting path, we have questioned and faltered. And so, we have worked hard and persisted. But we should always embrace the chance to learn from every situation. For example, Christopher's experience had a cognitive impact on Glad Tidings Church. He played a crucial role in shaping the parishioners into the leaders they are today. The young man's kindness pushed them to do their best, regardless of their curl treatment of him.

Now the question is for us! Have you ever been in a hopeless and stressful situation, wondering if things would change? You were so helpless that finding a solution seemed impossible? Despite your attempts, external circumstances prevented your advancement. Two words for you: "But GOD!" Nothing is impossible with The LORD

(Luke 1:37). No matter what challenges confront us. The Holy Spirit will always guide and comfort us (2 Corinthians 1:3-14).

"Thus, if anyone is in Christ, he is a new creation; old things have passed away, and look, new things have come. Everything is from GOD. He brought us back to Himself through Christ. And he gave us the ministry of reconciliation." 2 Corinthians 5:17-18. Holiness follows the writer's salvation and the renewal of his being in Christ. Hence, he experienced a complete transformation in his outlook on the world.

The Bible is free from confusion. Christians are "Not of the World." We still have battles to face (Jn 17:14-15). But as supporters of (Jesus), the Author and Perfecter of Our Faith (Hebrews. 12:2), We fight spiritual battles beyond comprehending other struggles. Thus, the Saints, day and night, are in spiritual warfare with the devil (Ephesians 6:10-11). Plus, our flesh is fighting back its old nature without a break (Galatians 5:16).

We may lose friends, family, and things we once desired from our old lives. But Jesus is the only influence in our life who still accepts us despite all our flaws. No matter what we do, obstacles will always present themselves along the way. Yet, it does not mean we must face them on our own or overcome them with no support.

Obstacles are inevitable; they will always be a part of the Christian walk. We will face many difficulties and find obstacles in every corner. These challenges will slow us down. If we do not proceed with care, they may block our growth in faith and hinder our walk with Christ.

Yet, we can also see setbacks as new chances for personal growth. They help us gain valuable knowledge. Through opposition experiences, GOD allows us to mature in our faith and learn to rely on Him daily (James 1:2-4). The Father never promised us a life free of problems. But He promised He would always be there for us (Isaiah 41:13) and never leave or forsake us (Deuteronomy 31:6).

Problems are unfamiliar and complex, which we dislike. New adversities scare us.

However, the writer defines a challenge—as a confrontation to establish superiority in ability or strength.

What are ways to develop a mindset unafraid of fresh problems? We can boost our confidence by approaching complex, challenging, unknown, and uncertain tasks. Although daunting, embracing new oppositions can lead to personal growth. However, most individuals experience fear when confronted with it. Embrace new and confrontational experiences to conquer fear. New conflicts are full of danger and worries. Nonetheless, the rewards are great when we overcome them. As we conquer fear, it increases confidence and boosts self-esteem.

Humans can think, communicate, and imagine. But it is a unique experience when we get involved. Nothing can replace our expertise. The best way to learn not to fear recent problems is to face them. Instead of procrastinating, it is better to confront new hardships. The more you expose yourself to new oppositions, the less fear you will have towards them.

Yet, some Christians remain fearful of any form of change. Complexity breeds worries and doubts, so we avoid it. That is why most Christians fear new struggles. They dislike uncertainty. Yet, a fearless attitude will make us less frightened when facing new adversities.

Commit and dedicate yourself by tracking your actions in this endeavor. One clever way to conquer additional difficulties is to keep a diary. In it, jot down actions taken and the outcomes. Access to this data will give you a clear view of your mistakes. It will make it easier to fix them.

Many problems stem from underdeveloped and unintegrated personalities. It is like walking through a pitch-black room, unable to see what is in front of you. Those lacking integration or development fear uncertainty, complexity, and hardships. Building a solid personality fosters adaptability, flexibility, proactivity, and courage in overcoming challenges.

CHAPTER 6

With unwavering faith in GOD, worrying about the future is unnecessary. He oversees everything. Just give it your all. Faith can be a source of strength and resilience in navigating life's challenges.

Trust Your Faith

Regardless of problems, we must approach them with a positive mindset. Faith in GOD's plan is crucial. It helps us overcome challenges and turn them into opportunities for growth. Faithfulness is a process that shapes our character. Still, uncertainty often triggers fear as our initial response.

It is possible to argue that anxiety displays a large naturalness. Over the years, the writer has realized that the unknown is critical. It fosters his fears and curiosity. It draws him to venture into uncharted territories and strive for greatness.

As stated by Romans 8:28, Christians should never fear problems. Trust they are a possibility. The LORD has sent them so the Glorified can learn something new and assess their smarts. Note this can be hard with deadlines and pressure. Still, we must trust in Christ. He atoned for our sins. So, faith will make each issue less scary.

The author speaks from experience—one who lived through ill health. Worldwide diseases and emotional distress are imminent. Yet sickness can cause anxiety, sleep problems, and depression-like symptoms. But nothing in the Bible says GOD stopped healing people when the writers completed it. The Gospels show Jesus was en route to heal someone or had healed (Mark 5:21–24, 35–43). It tells us that GOD is a healer by nature. Healing is an inherent characteristic of His Being.

For instance, Doctor Bingham was the lead pastor of the Church (Glad Tidings) in St. Louis, Missouri. A woman named Eliza was one of his parishioners. Her life, marked by chronic illness since childhood, was a testament to resilience.

Eliza's earliest memories had the clean scent of hospitals. They also had the hushed murmurs of concerned doctors. At the tender age of seven, doctors diagnosed her with a rare autoimmune disorder that left her frail. Hospital beds confined Eliza while machines and fluorescent lights surrounded her.

Despite her illness, Eliza sought comfort in her Bible and books. They took her to distant lands. These places sparked her mind with bright colors and endless adventures. She discovered resilience in the pages of the Bible and her favorite novels. She often talked about her nonfictional heroes in the Holy Writ. Despite facing impossible odds, they remained steadfast in their courage and faith.

Eliza's illness waxed and waned, granting temporary relief before resurging with greater intensity. This girl refused to let her illness define her. So, she embraced each setback as a challenge to conquer. She saw pain as a hurdle to leap over with unwavering determination.

Despite her health limits, Eliza pursued her education with joy. She devoured knowledge like a thirsty traveler finding an oasis. Her studies displayed her sharp and honed mind, shaped by adversity. Regardless of her body's limitations, she dreamed of reaching the stars.

But not her intellect that set Eliza apart; it was her indomitable, righteous Spirit. Her refusal to surrender to despair is a testament as she faces insurmountable odds. She approached each day with faithful grace. The young lady smiled, a beacon of hope in a world shrouded in darkness.

Despite the whispers of doubt that echoed in the recesses of her mind, Eliza refused to give up on her dreams. Still, she fought. The young girl pushed herself past her limits. She did this in pursuit of a future she had dared to imagine for herself.

Then, one fateful day, after years of struggle and sacrifice, Eliza won. Against all odds, she graduated from St. Louis University with top honors. Her name is in history. It proves that resilience and determination are robust.

As she stood on the threshold of a new chapter in her life, Eliza looked back on her journey with a sense of awe and wonder. She faced illness storms and emerged resilient.

Her spirit remained unbroken, a beacon of hope, despite her battered body. Illness did not define Eliza. What did was her strength and the profound faith GOD gave her.

So, GOD's people are to "Count it all joy, my brothers, when you face trials of various kinds. You know that evaluating your faith makes you steadfast. Let steadfastness have its full effect. Then, you will be perfect and complete, lacking nothing" (James 1:2-4).

The Apostle urges his readers not to give up when faced with challenges. Instead, he encourages them to allow perseverance to lead them to spiritual maturity. It underscores the significance of endurance and determination in the faith journey.

Like Paul, Apostle James emphasizes the power of perseverance. It is the power of staying strong when faced with challenges. We can grow a deeper faith as we endure trials with joy and determination. Thus, confronting and beating challenges can refine a person's character. It also strengthens their bond with GOD.

Faithful leaders teach us GOD's purposes for hardships and how they shape virtue. Hardships help us overcome problems. The Bible also teaches us that stumbling blocks can help us find joy in our sufferings. But acknowledging and embracing challenges is the first step. They include breakups, illness, and death.

As the Glorified endure hardships and challenges, it builds a solid faith. This idea is part of the Bible's motif of perseverance. In demanding times, it is crucial to have faith in GOD's purpose. These trials should serve a higher purpose in the believer's growth.

Investigating suffering may seem dark. But it is often the only path to enlightenment. Dark moments often result from mistakes or misjudgments. Yet, these mistakes can be valuable learning experiences. The lessons are challenging and painful. Yet, they can lead to growth. They create a more resilient, self-aware, and compassionate self. The Saints find strength and wisdom in The LORD as they embrace their darkest days for growth.

One example of this is when we make a mistake, as it shines a spotlight on areas where we may lack faith or skill. Yet, slipups can help us understand where to focus our efforts. Errors are an inherent component of acquiring knowledge. Mistakes show where to improve. These incidents arise because of insufficient knowledge or a deficit in skills.

Mistakes do not deter seasoned Saints. They view these experiences as essential building blocks for personal growth. Our guidance comes from them. They show us the areas that need more attention.

When the Saints acknowledge errors, it improves their ability to solve problems. It also helps them bounce back from setbacks. So, their faith fosters a mentality that embraces personal and professional growth. In this mindset, people see challenges as chances to learn and grow. They do not see them as failures. As the Saints see mistakes as steppingstones, learning can lead to a deeper understanding. Faith can improve personal and professional growth.

Mistakes often lead to the need for problem-solving. This process can lead to personal growth. It also brings better methods and more knowledge in distinct aspects of life. So, as believers develop critical thinking skills, creativity is possible through Biblical problem-solving.

"The simple believes everything, but the prudent think of his steps." Proverbs 14:15.

People of faith believe that, when faced with tragedy, they must focus on their beliefs. They must also improve their connection with Jesus. As the Bible states (1 John 5:4), "For everyone born of GOD overcomes the world. And this victory has overcome the world—our faith."

So, the GOD approach helps them become better people. They can then benefit society more. But praise and prayer preparation is essential before confronting hardships. So, Christians believe their faith can be comfort. It also gives resilience and purpose in adversity.

Admiration can boost one's self-esteem and confidence. When we trust our GOD-given abilities, we are more likely to face tough times with hope. To navigate difficulties, embrace worship, and stay rooted in the Sacred reality.

The Saints expressing admiration can affect the giver and receiver. It creates a positive, supportive environment. However, their faith adds to a sense of affirmation and encouragement. People often believe in one's abilities because of self-esteem and confidence. It can help people face challenges with resilience and optimism.

That said, Christianity involves many other righteous aspects. But believers must recognize their connection to Christ's death and resurrection. Christian Holiness is essential. We put our trust in them to get into fellowship with (Jesus), the Alpha and Omega. Yet, the Christian faith and its influence on our lives are much more than those core beliefs.

The Christian culture has a captivating history. It has worked hard to keep many rituals and artifacts. Jesus first became the focus of the Glorified. They have inherited and cherished his beliefs. In Christianity, GOD takes on human form and experiences the full range of humanity. At this moment, enlightenment reaches its peak. Other religions, unlike it, stress the importance of human effort in attaining Divinity.

So, the core belief in Jesus Christ as the Son of GOD is the Hallmark of Christianity. Christians trust that after the Last Judgment, The LORD will destroy all evil angels. He will also destroy all unsaved humans. This group includes Satan. But for now, the Bible says a Christian community is essential. Paul wrote in Galatians 6:2, "Help each other's burdens to fulfill the Law of Christ."

Faithful people should develop their spiritual gifts. These will strengthen their bond with the Church. It will also deepen their commitment to the Christian faith. The author has listed nine key attributes below. These can help ground Christianity during tough times. When followed, they give the Saints extra grace and help them stay afloat. They have let the writer engage with a supportive Christian community. They have also given the writer accountability and maturity.

Further, your friends and family can offer support and lend an ear during grim times. Yet, seeking help from a licensed therapist can provide crucial guidance. They can offer resources to build resilience. However, it is not advisable to burden a friend with the role of a therapist. Instead, a licensed Christian counselor can be an unbiased resource. They can help you investigate your life, check your struggles, and move you toward healing.

Friends and family can be a crucial support system. However, they may lack the training or objectivity needed. They cannot offer the level of guidance of a licensed therapist. It is essential to recognize the limits of personal relationships. Do not burden friends or family by expecting them to be a therapist.

Christian counseling integrates psychology with Christian faith and values. It provides an integrated approach for those who see faith as central to their lives. We are purpose-driven Christians. We know how important it is to use shared values to bring our faith to life. In tough times, this is especially valid. To help Christ's supporters, the nine concepts below represent our values. They are our promises to our LORD and Savior.

We must build connections with the people and the communities we serve in our daily walk. Each moral choice strengthens those bonds. It helps create a brand we can be proud of ourselves.

1. We should follow moral and ethical principles. They show how believers should live. It includes love, compassion, forgiveness, honesty, and justice teachings. Paul writes to the Church in Rome 13:8-10. "You must not commit adultery, murder, do not steal, and you must not covet." There may be other commands, too. They are all in this command: "Love your neighbor as yourself." Love does not harm a neighbor.

2. Note that community fellowship plays a significant role in the lives of believers. It provides a sense of belonging, support, and association. It fosters unity among the Christian laity. "I appeal to you, brothers, by Our Lord Jesus Christ. I ask you to agree and strive for unity in the same mind and judgment. Do this with no divisions among you." 1 Corinthians 1:10.

3. Christians should serve others in charity and kindness. Our good works let others see our charitable deeds. They glorify GOD and live out Jesus' teachings. These teachings emphasize caring for the less fortunate. "Pure religion before GOD The Father is this: to visit orphans and widows when they suffer. Also, to keep oneself clean from the world." James1: twenty-seven.

4. Christ supporters must include prayer and worship, regardless of challenging seasons. As we gather for communal devotion, add prayer. It will help us build a deeper faith and relationship with GOD. Like your parents, your Heavenly Father wants to talk with you. He also wants to guide and support you.

As the Saints pray, The Father listens, and we can know His presence in the silence. The Author of Salvation (Hebrews 2:10) answers our prayers. He does this through thoughts, spiritual experiences, passages from Scripture, or others' actions. Jesus' speaking: "You may ask me for anything in my name, and I will do it..." John 14:13-14.

5. We cannot pass over daily Scripture study of the Old and New Testaments. These are the Holy Books of Christianity. For Christians to study the Sacred Texts, it is essential to understand Jesus' teachings and the history of the faith. The Bible shows us its transformative power. It emphasizes that the Word of GOD is not another book.

   It is a living force that can change individuals from the inside out. "For the Word of GOD is alive and active. The Word is sharper than any double-edged sword. It even divides the soul and spirit, joints and marrow. It judges the thoughts and attitudes of the heart." Hebrews 4:12.

6. Stained glass and air conditioning sanctuaries cannot convert lost souls alone. Thus, mission and evangelism must spread the Gospel. They do this by sharing their faith and the message of salvation with others.

   Christian evangelism fulfills the Great Commission. Jesus told his disciples to make disciples of all nations. See Matthew 28:18-20. The prophet Isaiah wrote, "GOD's Word that comes from our mouth will not return to us empty. It will do what He wants and achieve His purpose." Isaiah 55:11

7. We must never forget our faith calls for Personal Growth and Transformation. It emphasizes that the Saints seek to become like Christ. They do this in their character and actions. Begin your journey right from the place where you find yourself. Start by feeding yourself milk before you jump to solid food.

You will get there. Just let yourself grow into it. "Like newborn babies, they crave pure spiritual milk. It will help you grow in your salvation. You have tasted that The LORD is good." 1 Peter 2:2-3.

8. GOD's people must keep the essential rituals like baptism, communion, and confession. It keeps communication open if trouble arises. The sacraments are a paradigm that reminds us why we must stay faithful and unified. As believers communicate in sacraments, they build solid Christian relationships.

   "Have they not informed you that those we baptized into Christ Jesus, we did it unto his death? We buried them in water and raised them to life. It was so that The Father raised Christ from the dead by His great power. We did it so we too might walk in the new life." Study Romans 6:3-4.

9. We all know how important Education and Scholarship are. So, Christians must continue their traditions, rich scholarship, and theological reflection history. We must continue to lead in philosophy, theology, science, and other fields. The Bible verse 2 Timothy 2:15 advises us to study and show GOD our diligent comprehension of the truth.

   The young pastor, Timothy, focuses on understanding GOD's Word and spotting false teachings. Biblical knowledge is vital in Christian Education. Take pride in being a student. Make the most of your academic journey. Give your best effort and always strive for excellence.

CHAPTER 7

Visitors will never love a Worship Center until the parishioners love it foremost.

Cultural Building

Christianity is diverse. It has many cultures and denominations. So, the emphasis on the above chapter's nine bullet points may vary. It is valid among denominational groups. Interpretations of theology may cause doctrinal differences. So, because of cultural contrasts in interpreting beliefs. Yet, be polite and respect their explanation. Acknowledge that their Scripture interpretation includes reasonable points.

Liz Fosslien writes: "Diversity has a seat at the table. Inclusion has a voice. Having that voice heard is belonging."

For example, something like this: "Your take on that Bible Passage makes a good point. Your comment gives me some food for thought." A moderate tone is imperative to avoid appearing aggressive. Remember the impact of your facial expressions and be aware of the signals you send. Note that paying attention and respecting someone's perspective is critical. Do this without criticizing it, even if you disagree. It can affect them and you beyond question.

You will engage in civil discourse, which is vital for Scripture sharing.

That said, Maya was a close friend of the writer. She owned a restaurant called Harmony in historic South St. Louis. She was an enthusiastic young woman. Maya believed in serving tasty coffee and pastries. But it was also a hub of cultural exchange and community building.

Maya valued diversity. She had a multicultural upbringing. She grasped the need to encourage understanding between people of diverse backgrounds.

One sunny morning, while serving coffee to a customer. Maya noticed an article on the front page. It advertised an upcoming cultural festival celebrating South St. Louis's diverse heritage. The idea inspired Maya to turn her restaurant into a small cultural hub. It happened before the festival.

She invited customers to share stories, traditions, and even recipes from their cultures. Soon, her coffee shop buzzed with conversations in different languages. The air carried the aroma of spices from various cuisines.

A regular customer named Javier is a Spanish artist. He volunteered to host a weekly art workshop. There, patrons can explore art from around the world. Maya also invited local musicians to perform live music representing various cultural genres.

As days passed, her shop became more than a place to grab coffee. The town became a melting pot of cultures. People from all walks came together to learn, share, and connect.

One memorable evening, Maya organized a storytelling night. People could share folktales and anecdotes from their homelands. Laughter, tears, and storytelling filled the restaurant, transcending language barriers.

The cultural festival finally arrived, and Maya was at the heart of the celebration. Her efforts paid off, as her shop symbolized unity and acceptance in the community.

Case in point, our Churches must not remain segregated on Sunday mornings. Maya realized that culture was not about traditions and customs. Christians should know the Church is about uniting people from diverse backgrounds. The local congregation should become a testament to the power of Matthew 28:18-20. Culture building through Christian prayers in every sermon. It will remind every parishioner of the beauty of diversity. Open hearts and minds will keep cultural exchange alive in Christianity.

Also, meaningful discussions about Scripture or any other subject rely on peaceful debate. Polite conversation involves respectful and open dialogue. It lets individuals share their beliefs and opinions. They do so while listening to and considering others' perspectives. Sharing Scripture is crucial. Beliefs about spiritual texts differ among people. Respectful discussions help people share ideas better. They foster understanding and respect.

Essential components of respectful dialogue comprise the six bullet points below:

1. Using respectful language. Avoid offensive or inflammatory words that might hinder constructive conversation.
2. Listen to others. Try to understand their views before responding.
3. Be open to different interpretations and viewpoints. Recognize that people may approach Scripture with diverse backgrounds, experiences, and beliefs.
4. If you disagree with a viewpoint, express your disagreement non-threatening. Focus on the ideas. Do not attack the person saying them.
5. Identify areas of agreement or shared understanding. It can help build bridges and create a more harmonious dialogue.
6. If something is unclear, ask for more information. Thus, this will help you understand one's perspective. Do not make assumptions.

When the Saints apply these ideas, they can make Scripture-sharing talks more effective. They can foster understanding and unity among people with diverse beliefs.

Still, the dogma distinction interbred with human traditions. Thus, it can be challenging, leading to division and conflict among the faithful. These serve no practical purpose. Individuals engaging in Church traditions and sacraments, not as we do, are burdensome. It is especially so when they do not interpret them as we do.

In Jesus' day, it was even so with the Pharisees. He forgave, healed, and socialized with outcasts, challenging Temple practices. All were acts of compassion and grace. But His methods threatened the established social traditions.

Ruth Bader Ginsburg wrote: "Whatever you choose to do, leave tracks." Case in point, We should want to leave the world better, for we have lived. It underscores the importance of affecting and leaving a meaningful legacy. She suggests that one's actions should not be for personal gain or fulfillment. They should also help to improve the world or society. By leaving tracks, one leaves a mark. It is a trail of beneficial influence that will inspire or benefit others.

Ms. Ginsburg's statement prompts people to think more with skill. She also encourages us to reason wider open. It shows dedication to leaving a lasting, positive impact on the world. It ensures that future generations can enjoy the work. They can appreciate the achievements of their predecessors. The idea is to strive for a lasting, positive impact beyond individual goals. It reflects a commitment to leave the world better than one found it.

Scriptures Twisting Causes Problems

To twist the Scriptures is to separate GOD's Word from its context. It means turning it into their interpretation. A person, congregation, or denomination would do this on purpose. They twist the Scriptures to promote their wrong traditions. It empowers them to hold a steadfast conviction in their agnostic teachings.

But Evangelical Theologians see this as a misinterpretation. It involves taking passages out of their intended context. Then, people alter them to suit beliefs or agendas. Wrong doctrine is challenging for the Local Churches.

So, avoiding using a Passage of Scripture out of context is vital. It can lead to errors and misunderstandings. Yet, sometimes, this is not the case. We can present a verse as a standalone quote. But that does not show misuse. We take it from its original backdrop. The verses reveal a standalone truth. Others need their context to interpret and apply them.

Case in point: believers often quote John 3:16 alone. Yet, it is crucial to grasp the context. Jesus spoke these words during his talk with Nicodemus. The LORD and Nicodemus talked about being born again and GOD's plan for salvation.

In John's Chapter Three, the context of their conversation shows this. So, taking John 3:16 from the Passage does not change its meaning. This verse's constant sense justifies removing it from its context.

Yet, Jeremiah 29:11 is not a standalone verse. "I know My plans for you," emphasizes The LORD. "They are to help you, not to harm you. They are to give you hope and a future." However, free-thinking Christians consider any Passage a literal statement by the author. They do not do so unless they intend to create an allegory, poetry, or other genres.

The narcissists believe everything revolves around them. They think it means GOD will fulfill all their dreams. They believe their lives achieve happiness and success. What is the outcome when we cannot get everything we desire? What are the consequences if we experience harm and lack of prosperity?

Remember, the vivid details near the text can change the Bible study experience. When we understand Jeremiah's Chapter 29, we find it is a Letter. It is complete with wisdom and guidance. But to our disappointment, the prophet did not write it for a private purpose.

The "You" in this letter refers to a group of people. They are the exiled Jews to whom Jeremiah writes. For Hananiah, his false prophecies echoed through the minds of the disillusioned. Despite the irony, Hananiah prophesied prosperity for the Jews. He assured them it would come to pass in two years.

In Chapter 29, Jeremiah refutes a false prophecy. The writer also paints a bleak picture of the Jews' future. He reveals they would endure over seventy years without freedom. He warned them a lot about the results of disobeying GOD's commands. Note that during the seventy years of exile, they proved him right.

The false doctrine includes any belief or teaching not stated in the Bible. The Apostle John shared what to do about those who teach misleading ideas. In II John 1:10, John advises not to welcome or wish well someone who rejects this doctrine."

Still, many people do it. They keep their human beliefs and views. Yet, the problem is that religions often confuse and misinterpret the original teachings. Misinterpretations create difficulties on many righteous levels.

These challenges cause issues in many areas. They affect personal relationships, social cohesion, and ethics. That said, misunderstandings can sometimes fuel the growth of intolerance, discrimination, or conflict.

So, context is crucial. It is vital to understanding the true meaning of any text, including the Holy Scriptures. Yet, twisting the Scriptures can misrepresent passages. It promotes ideas that may not align with the intended message of the Sacred texts. This practice can add to theological confusion. Erroneous Doctrine can cause division and spread misinformation in religious communities.

Resolving misleading dogma requires creating an open environment. It needs advocacy for Christian Education and empathy. Also, the Church fosters critical thinking. It does this in its small groups, Bible study, and preaching. Theological scholars, devout leaders, and individuals play crucial roles. They reexamine and clarify interpretations. They do this to align them with their traditions' original teachings and values.

Many Christian denominations stress studying the Scriptures. It means considering history, culture, language, and the text's message. Scholars and Church leaders often stress the need for responsible and accurate interpretation. The correct interpretation is to avoid the pitfalls of misunderstanding the Holy Writ. Or to twist the Scriptures for personal or ideological gain.

Some traditions have positives. But it is disheartening to see group leaders abuse these customs. They also used them to allow discrimination and limit wider freedoms. The LORD often rebuked the religious leaders. "You nullify the Word of GOD by your tradition that you have handed down" (Mark 7:13).

In Jesus' day, ordinary people felt confused and helpless. Many changes to GOD's Law by the traditions of the scribes and Pharisees caused this. Jesus quoted Isaiah in Mark 7:6–8, calling them religious hypocrites. "You have let go of GOD's commands and are holding onto human traditions." The LORD's critique focused on leaders valuing traditions more than GOD's commands. It highlighted the importance of mercy. It also stressed the importance of compassion and sincerity. These are important in one's connection with the Divine.

But it confuses churchgoers. Mixing "Decrees of men" with Divine "Doctrines" leads to misunderstandings. The problem arises from this situation. Like oil and water, do not mix. Romans 6:18 stresses, "This is how we know the children of GOD and the children of the devil. Whoever does not do right is not of GOD. Nor is the one who does not love his brother." 1 John 3:10. Jesus said we invalidate and void the Gospel. So, it has no effect when humans add to their practices.

It would help if you considered the context and interpretation of such verses. They are part of the larger Biblical narrative and theology.

Different Christian denominations may interpret these passages. So, understanding the historical and cultural context is crucial for complete comprehension.

"Thus, making the Word of GOD void by the tradition you have handed down. And many such things you do." Mark 7:13. In this context, Jesus addresses religious leaders. They focused on their traditions and rituals. The religious leaders did not concentrate on the genuine Spirit of GOD's commandments. The writer's Passage emphasizes the importance of true devotion to the Almighty's teachings. It is over human traditions.

So, the comprehensive view of salvation must expand. It must do so regardless of one's fear of danger. We are followers of Christ. We must speak up and spread the Gospel without fear. Only our conduct cannot show others the knowledge of Christ. So, living like Christ is essential. But believers must also share the Gospel through words and actions. Salvation and the message of Christ's sacrifice are vital. They guide others to a relationship with GOD.

Culture Learning

Christians should learn from every culture. Without cultural awareness, we are more likely to misjudge people from other cultures. A lack of cultural awareness causes many challenges. It hinders effective communication and understanding of people's motives.

By valuing cultural awareness, Christians and people can build bridges between communities. Respect for different beliefs enhances dialogue. Intercultural dialogue promotes global awareness. Ethnic diversity bridges the gaps between diverse cultures by exchanging views.

It is crucial to cultivate cultural awareness. It connects communities through understanding, respect, and dialogue. For example, it unites

Christians with people from diverse backgrounds. Cultural awareness can contribute to bridge-building.

Multicultural awareness helps people understand diverse values, beliefs, and customs. Christians can understand the world better by learning about many cultures. It will deepen their understanding and appreciation of diversity. For example:

Promoting Mutual Respect: Valuing others' cultural diversity is crucial. It helps create an inclusive and accepting society.

(2) Christians can respect people of diverse faiths and customs. They do this by embracing cultural awareness and fostering acceptance.

(3) Understanding unfamiliar cultures is crucial for fostering meaningful conversations between faiths. Christians can discuss with people from diverse backgrounds. They can find common ground. They can share experiences and explore similarities between their faith and others.

(4) Being aware of diverse cultures helps foster authentic connections. Saints seek knowledge and appreciation for diverse cultures. They are more likely to make good connections. They will also shatter stereotypes and nurture unity.

(5) The Glorified promotes peace and harmony. Self-composedness requires a deep understanding of and respect for distinct cultures. Christians accepting diversity can help a lot. It can create a more connected and empathetic world.

(6) As we know many cultures, we can confront and beat prejudice and misunderstandings. Christians can promote understanding and learning. They can do this by having open conversations. These conversations should address misconceptions about their faith. They should also offer chances to learn about others' beliefs and practices.

(7) Pursuing social justice causes a deep appreciation and awareness of diverse cultures. Love and compassion guide Christians. They can help solve social issues that affect unfamiliar cultures and religions. They advocate for equality and justice.

(8) Rather than viewing differences as obstacles, cultural awareness encourages celebrating diversity. Christians make society more dynamic. They do this by joining in events, festivals, and activities. These things highlight diverse cultures.

Once more, Christians and people from diverse backgrounds can build unity. They can do this by embracing cultural awareness. And by building fellowship bridges and engaging in meaningful dialogue.

The Saints learn about the customs and traditions of different ethnic groups. Communication helps them have meaningful talks. It lets them build relationships with people from diverse backgrounds. Then, teaching all people the concepts of righteousness. The Bible promotes a mindset of being right. And the practical use of Christian principles. It stresses the need for ongoing learning and growth. It is paramount across cultures and denominations.

As we look back on the time's history, religion and politics made it tough to accept Jesus as LORD. Plus, He challenged the established religious norms of his time. That did not help His situation. Jesus said He was the Messiah and GOD's Son. He said He fulfilled Old Testament prophecies. His claim only added to His problems.

Also, Jesus' non-traditional teachings often contradicted the Jewish leaders' traditional interpretations. That made it challenging for many to accept Him as the promised Messiah. So, the Pharisees and Sadducees saw Jesus threatening their authority and influence. He proclaimed the kingdom's arrival and made threats against the Temple. The LORD challenged the idea that the kingdom was near. He hinted that He and His disciples would soon teach in it.

Judea was under Roman rule during Jesus' time. The Jewish people sought a Messiah. They believed He would free them from Roman oppression. He would also establish a Jewish kingdom. But Jesus' message was about a spiritual realm, not a political one. It disappointed many with original hopes for the Messiah. The LORD expected His followers to run from self-reliance and Jewish tradition. They were to run into His Father's arms. They would depend on His strength, not their norms.

Fear of Roman authorities discouraged many from following Jesus. Jewish leaders feared retaliation. Hence, loyalty to a new spiritual leader could incite rebellion. Roman Law would punish this rebellion against the state or monarch. So, they sought traditional norms. They feared rejection from the elders. Norms can simplify social interactions because they are robotic. But they can have terrible results when we copy lousy conduct.

Also, Jesus used parables and metaphors. They made it hard for some people to understand His teachings. His message was often counterintuitive and challenged conventional wisdom. So, joining the early Christian movement could lead to social isolation or persecution. Those who accepted Jesus as LORD risked alienation from their families and communities. The Jews continued to follow the traditional norms of their religious leaders.

But people often resist change, especially when it involves shifting their beliefs. Hence, letting go of old traditions is hard. Also, accepting a new faith leader can be challenging. People often have deep spiritual and personal connections with their faith leaders. They adjust to a new leader's style, personality, and teachings. It can be difficult. Change requires time, and patience is essential. Both faith leaders and congregants should expect a gradual transition.

Righteousness motivates individuals to confront biases and cultivate empathy. So, seizing diversity is critical to growth in Local Church communities. Christians embracing diversity can lead to personal development within the Church. It encourages people to face biases, broaden their perspectives, and cultivate empathy.

As evangelicals, we will face many challenges. Individuals of any belief system will face them. These challenges can be both internal and external. Challenges and difficulties are part of human norms, regardless of spiritual affiliation. Yet, Christianity provides a framework for addressing and finding meaning in these challenges. You must seek guidance. It should come from trusted spiritual figures. Christian counseling is crucial for complex issues.

But young and older adults can offer valuable insights and wisdom. Wisdom is not dependent on age. Young people often bring fresh perspectives. They have innovative ideas and a unique understanding of today's issues. Their experiences, challenges, and successes give them wisdom. It is different and relevant to the current times—more about this in the next chapter.

CHAPTER 8

Acceptance and inclusion of distinct cultures define a diverse society. It is receptive, willing to listen, observe, engage in conversation, and embrace other cultures while preserving its own.

Inclusiveness

I f a Saint or anybody is searching for truth and inner peace, the writer recommends practicing self-awareness, pursuing knowledge, and consulting with Christian authorities for guidance. It is common for individuals to find solace and guidance through their faith, and it is highly beneficial to seek support from wise and mature individuals who are part of the Glorified realm community.

Christianity's communal support can be invaluable and encouraging, providing shared experiences and a sense of belonging on the spiritual journey regardless of age or culture. Too, Christian's collaborative support creates an environment where individuals can spiritually, emotionally, and socially thrive despite struggles.

Life has many challenges, and a community with shared values and beliefs can offer emotional support during challenging times. Besides spirituality, the Christian community should participate in various social activities, events, and outreach programs. These activities allow individuals to interact, network, and collaborate, leading to a diverse and satisfying social life.

One unique aspect of Christian communities is their intergenerational nature. People of different ages and life stages come together, offering a wealth of experiences and wisdom. This intergenerational connection can enrich and give a broader perspective on faith and life. Thus, being part of a Christian community allows individuals to share their spiritual experiences, struggles, and triumphs. Shared understanding creates a sense of unity and helps people realize they are not alone during challenging seasons or on the faith journey.

Likewise, Philippians 2:2-3, "Do nothing out of selfish ambition or vain conceit. Rather, in humility, value others above yourselves, not looking to your interests but each of you to the interests of the others." The Apostle's teaching promotes a selfless and compassionate attitude, encouraging individuals to cultivate a mindset that seeks the good of others. It reflects the Christian principle of loving one's neighbor and exemplifies the virtues of humility and putting others before ourselves.

Taking Children Seriously

The writer's cousin often talks about a wise older man named Mr. Tobias.

People admired Tobias. They admired him for his kindness, gentle nature, and profound respect for children.

Unlike many adults in his religious community, he has a unique perspective. They saw children as mere novelties or lesser beings. But Tobias saw them as valuable members of righteousness. He believed they held a wisdom and innocence that adults often overlooked. And so, whenever a child spoke, Tobias listened.

One sunny morning, Tobias sat outside his home. He was enjoying the sun's warmth on his weathered face. A group of children skipped to his steps. Their laughter filled the air like music.

"Good morning, Mr. Tobias!" Excitement filled their eyes as they chorused.

"Good morning, my young friends," Tobias greeted them with a warm smile. "What brings you to my home?"

The eldest of the group, Lily, stepped forward, her eyes shining with determination. We need your help, Mr. Tobias. The stream where the animals drink has dried up, and they cannot drink.

Mr. Tobias nodded, stroking his long white beard. He emphasizes, "That is a problem." "We said we are concerned about that problem." "But you have the solution."

The children exchanged puzzled glances, but Tobias smiled and beckoned them closer. He led them to a grove of ancient oak trees, where a small spring bubbled up from the earth.

Tobias spoke, his voice a blend of tenderness and determination, as he urged them to listen. "The answers you seek are all around you if only you know how to listen."

The children watched as Tobias kneeled by the spring. His hands cupped the clear water. "Every drop of water is precious," his voice filled with conviction and urgency. No matter how small, every voice deserves to be heard, like any other voice.

Tobias's words inspired the children. With their youthful energy and creativity, they embarked on devising a plan. They gathered buckets and barrels. They weaved through the forest like a merry band of adventurers. And with each step, they listened—to the rustle of leaves, the chirping of birds, and the murmur of the wind.

Jesus spoke, "Let the little children come to me, and do not hinder them, for the kingdom of heaven belongs to such as these." Matthew 19:14 — The New International Version (NIV).

Besides, Jesus emphasized in Matthew 28:18-20 that His Great Commission is for everyone, as He mentioned "Every creature" and "All nations." The verses tell us that besides the inclusiveness of multicultural individuals, having children, especially in worship, encourages us to examine how we engage in Holy reverence, faith, and each other. Therefore, the Church should recognize young Christians as essential members and include them on an equal footing with others.

As per GOD's Word, there are no references to the "Children's Church" or youth minister. Today's Christians accept teaching children the Bible appropriately for their age and understanding. However, there are a lot of benefits to adding children's ministry to a Church. Nevertheless, many parents and religious educators find value in instilling moral and ethical teachings from the Holy Writs without the help of the Children's Church.

Still, the youth ministry can be a valuable tool for connecting with peers and forming healthy friendships to learn about GOD on their level, develop good morals and standards, and get closer to people who follow The LORD. Youth ministries often use creative and engaging methods to teach Biblical principles, making them more accessible and relatable for teenagers. However, parents should enforce what they learn at Church by preparing and teaching it at home.

Yet, it is crucial to approach the Children's Church with respect and sensitivity. We must be careful not to belittle or judge young Christians based on their understanding of Christian concepts. It can negatively affect children's connections with their peers, teachers, and families. When children sense inadequacy, they can manifest in behaviors like a lack of motivation or a reluctance to have faith in GOD.

He was a youth pastor many years ago, so the writer knows children have many questions about life and what to expect for the future. So, he encouraged a nurturing and inclusive environment where he welcomed the questions that could help them develop a healthy relationship with GOD and build their faith. He also promoted an open dialogue and encouraged group discussions, where children could share their thoughts and learn from each other. It showed them the value of being part of the Christian community and shared righteous exploration.

Mature believers should always model an atmosphere of curiosity for young adults. It shows a curious and open-minded attitude toward your faith. So, let your actions show that even uncomfortable questions are welcome; this sets an example for children and shows them that questioning is a natural part of life and spiritual growth.

Therefore, regardless of age, balancing teaching Christian values, promoting tolerance, and understanding diverse beliefs is essential for everyone. So, recognizing that individuals may have different perspectives and interpretations of faith can contribute to a more inclusive and respectful Holy community. It emphasizes the importance of fostering an inclusive and respectful community by balancing teaching Christian values with promoting tolerance and understanding diverse beliefs, regardless of age.

We must not overlook that young individuals undergo a transformative journey toward becoming devout Christians, encompassing their spiritual and physical growth. In an inclusive environment, we can learn how to disagree and strengthen our unity in the Body of Christ. Yet, showing bias towards any group in the congregation can harm our connections with those not part of our group.

In-group Bias

When the Local Church treats outsiders otherwise, it can result from our tendency to favor in-group members. In-group bias is the tendency to prefer insiders and treat outsiders differently. Within social psychology, in-group favoritism is the preference for same-group individuals and excluding outsiders. Understanding and addressing in-group bias is essential for promoting inclusivity, reducing discrimination, and fostering positive intergroup relations.

Inside-group bias can result from identity, shared experiences, and a desire for belonging. Stereotypes and prejudices develop when individuals overemphasize the positive traits of their group and hold negative views toward outsiders. Lack of trust is a significant barrier to reconciliation. It is often a spinoff of injustices, violence, or betrayal that has eroded trust between the Church's conflicting parties.

Yet, wisdom extends beyond the boundaries of maturity or leadership. It is why making sound judgments, applying knowledge, and approaching life's challenges with balance and understanding are all qualities often attributed to wisdom. As the Glorified recognizes, age does not define young and older Christians. We all have a distinct voice in Jesus Christ. This inclusive view of wisdom encourages a collaborative and open-minded approach to navigating life's complexities.

Everybody can develop wisdom through various experiences, self-reflection, and educational opportunities, regardless of age. While growing older and life experiences can contribute to gaining knowledge, people of any age can have valuable perspectives, emotional intelligence, and the ability to make thoughtful decisions. It highlights the importance of embracing diverse voices and experiences within the spiritual context.

As we recognize that wisdom is a constantly developing trait, it is crucial, as it means individuals have the potential to become wiser throughout their entire lives. So, as they open themselves up to learning, embracing diverse perspectives and cultivating self-awareness are crucial elements in the ongoing development of wisdom, regardless of one's age or level of maturity.

Besides, inter-generational collaboration or constructive interaction combines the youth's energy with the older adults' experience. This approach gains greater effectiveness by tapping into individuals' strengths and perspectives from different age groups. By working together, individuals can complement each other, leading to a more well-rounded and effective team. The constructive collaboration between youth's energy and older adults' experience creates a well-rounded and resilient Local Church better equipped to navigate the challenges of a transforming world.

Once again, young individuals typically bring enthusiasm, fresh ideas, and a willingness to embrace change. They may be technologically savvy, creative, and open-minded. However, older adults often possess a wealth of experience, accumulated knowledge, and a deep understanding of historical context. They may have developed strong critical thinking skills, emotional intelligence, and a long-term perspective.

Yet, a multi-generational Christian team can achieve a righteous, balanced, harmonious dynamic by bringing their talented attributes together to bring many challenges under control. The energy and creativity of young people can overcome traditional obstacles, while the wisdom and experience of older generations can offer guidance and valuable perspectives and avoid unnecessary errors. When Christians include multiculturalism, they can:

- Develop an ear to listen to the Holy Spirit
- Stop reasoning with the unreasonable
- Improve financial stewardship
- Put family first
- Prioritize distraction-free moments of solitude

As Church leaders combine, the youth's passion and older adults' wisdom create a formidable force. The Saints collaborating across age groups benefits the Local Church and outreach ministries. By acknowledging that each generation brings its own set of strengths, the faithful can harness the power of these diverse qualities to construct a Christian future that is both resilient and sustainable.

Christians have a shared responsibility to support and help each other. The writer of Hebrews advises us to inspire each other toward love and acts of goodness. Similarly, The LORD expects that younger individuals should willingly submit themselves to the guidance and authority of their elders. "Obey your leaders and submit to them, for they are watching your souls, as those who will have to give an account. Let them do this joyfully and not groaning, for that would be useless to you." Hebrews 13:17.

Let's consider if the Glorified individuals do not consistently submit to their Christian brethren. If so, they are speaking ill, defaming, disrespecting, insulting, undermining, dishonoring, and spreading false accusations against the Word of GOD. The Bible tells us afresh: "Do not let any unwholesome talk come out of your mouths, but only what helps build others up according to their needs, that it may benefit those who listen" (Ephesians 4:29).

Listen, Christians have a shared responsibility to support and help each other. The writers of the Bible have rooted them in various teachings found in the Holy Writ. The above quote is reminiscent of Biblical principles of love, mutual encouragement, and respect for authority. These Biblical principles collectively contribute to the idea that Christians have a shared responsibility to support and help each other, fostering a sense of community, compassion, and shared commitment to living out the teachings of the faith.

Case in point, the writer of Hebrews encourages believers to inspire one another toward love and acts of goodness. Many Biblical passages stress the value of love and doing good, and this aligns with them. The Apostle Paul frequently noted the significance of demonstrating love and virtuous behavior, as seen in Galatians 5:22-23. *"But the fruit of the Spirit is love, joy, peace, forbearance, kindness, goodness, faithfulness, gentleness and self-control. Against such things, there is no Law."*

So, the notion that younger individuals should willingly submit themselves to the guidance and authority of their elders reflects Biblical teachings on respect for authority and mentorship. Various passages, such as 1 Peter 5:5 and Titus 2:2-8, emphasize humility, respect for elders, and learning from the wisdom of those more experienced in the faith. These passages highlight the importance of humility, respect, and the passing down of wisdom from older individuals to the younger generation within the Christian faith.

The book of Titus, Chapter 2, verses 2-8 in the New International Version, also discusses mentorship and the responsibility of elders to guide the younger generation.

"Teach the older men to be temperate, worthy of respect, self-controlled, and sound in faith, love, and endurance. Likewise, teach the older women to be reverent in their lives, not slanderers or addicted to too much wine, but to teach what is good. Then they can urge the younger women to love their husbands and children, to be self-controlled and pure, to be busy at home, to be kind, and to be subject to their husbands so that no one will malign the Word of GOD."

"Similarly, encourage the young men to be self-controlled. In everything, set them an example by doing what is good. When conducting your teaching, demonstrate integrity, seriousness, and eloquence in your speech so that critics may be without valid grounds for reproach, resulting in embarrassment."

Submission is not blind obedience but a willingness to learn and benefit from the wisdom of others. Parents and elders should teach respect to the young through daily experiences. For example, they should compel a child to apologize for their mistakes or disrespectful behavior and emphasize the importance of imparting righteous values through practical lessons. It molds the child to adhere to regulations and comprehend the significance of respectful conduct in constructing a harmonious and interconnected society.

These teachings emphasize the interdependence of the Christian community and the need to cultivate a nurturing and caring atmosphere. Believers should support the Church community by encouraging each other, showing love through actions, and respecting experienced guidance, regardless of who they are.

Although the future is uncertain, planning is always wise. A forward-thinking approach is an intelligent way for parishioners to navigate uncertainty and make better-informed choices. Whether it is evangelism, mission, or Christian Education, having a well-thought-out plan can help the leadership master many challenges and offer a roadmap for achieving goals and adapting to changing circumstances.

Still, we will have our low points. But know we are not alone. Consider using the bullet points below during challenging seasons:

- I need some help and would appreciate your support.
- Take the time to acknowledge and connect with your innermost feelings.
- We are offering our support and hope that you will accept it.
- It is essential to lend a helping hand to those in need.
- Embrace a mindset of thinking significantly and reaching for the impossible.
- A positive mindset is critical to overcoming challenges and achieving personal growth.

An optimistic outlook is crucial for overcoming challenges and fostering personal growth. However, A positive mindset is not about ignoring or denying challenges but about facing them with resilience and optimism and approaching problems with a constructive and optimistic perspective. Therefore, cultivating an encouraging mentality is a continuous process that often requires self-awareness, mindfulness, and intentional efforts to shift one's thoughts toward the positive aspects of life. Life is a multifaceted experience, with many positive elements contributing to our well-being and fulfillment.

Here are a couple of reasons to appreciate life.

- Relationships
- Personal Growth
- Health and Well-being
- Nature and Beauty
- Creativity and Expression
- Learning and Education
- Joyful Experiences
- Gratitude and Mindfulness

CHAPTER 9

Those willing to take risks are likelier to find greater satisfaction and happiness. Our truth presents the most daunting challenge, forcing us to confront our deepest fears and vulnerabilities.

The Truth

Truth is a principle that has been the object of philosophical, scientific, and ethical examination for centuries. In its essence, truth denotes the quality or state of aligning with fact or reality. We separate it from falsehood or untruth, which includes statements or beliefs that do not match with the reality we experience. Our thoughts, morals, and cultural backgrounds shape our view of veracity realism.

Case in point, our mental picture influences the way we interpret events and the meaning we attribute to them. Christians need to understand how their minds interpret truth to communicate Holiness effectively. It also allows for personal growth in faith and spirituality. Thus, understanding how unfamiliar cultures interpret Biblical texts can improve communication. It encourages open and understanding discussions about living a life based on Divine principles and moral values.

Further, incorporating prayer and meditation into truth-telling can offer spiritual insight and guidance. Prayer can take many forms, and we can do it privately or in a communal setting. It may involve spoken or silent words, Holy reflection, visualization, or physical gestures. Prayer practice aids in establishing a stronger connection with the Divine. It clarifies moral or ethical concepts associated with being morally right or justifiable in one's actions or behavior.

So, we should use caution when confronting someone with a harsh or uncomfortable reality. People who consistently make immoral choices may not understand their realistic motivations. The facts of the truth to them can be like ripping off a bandage - painful but still necessary. For example, if you want to bake a cake, it is essential to have the required ingredients and follow the recipe. Prayer and Biblical principles enhance delivering substandard news.

In the short term, facing discomfort or pain can lead to better outcomes. Being honest and truthful is sometimes challenging. Despite these challenges, honesty and truthfulness are righteous qualities. These are guiding principles in the lives of GOD's people. Effective communication and healthy relationships require balancing truthfulness and consideration. However, considering others' feelings and well-being is essential.

Therefore, we should approach an unpleasant conversation with kindness and empathy. So, reflecting on how a painful situation would affect your emotions and thoughts is wise if reversed. It helps you gain insight into your (own) truthful motivations and the motivations of others. And so, you can make more discerning decisions that pave the way for achieving long-term goals for yourself and those around you. Afresh, when sharing not-so-great news, put yourself in their position.

When we show understanding and care for the person's feelings and perspective, it emphasizes we care about their well-being. Thus, positive energy evokes affirmative emotions and virtuous thoughts when tackling someone's issue. It adds authentic color to our perception of reality. For example, a person in a sunny mood may perceive a situation more positively than someone in a bad mood, even if the objective circumstances are the same. Individual experiences, traits, and support networks can influence different responses to a challenge.

Below are ten considerations when dealing with individuals misrepresenting the complete story.

1. Be kind and understanding when sharing the truth, and show compassion and empathy throughout the conversation. Use thoughtful and non-confrontational language.
2. Let the person know you intend to give unwavering support as they navigate their difficulties. Convey an atmosphere of understanding, and you are there to assist them in any way you can.
3. Select the perfect moment and location to reveal the truth. It is best not to broach sensitive topics in public or when someone is upset.
4. I do not mean to be redundant; show empathy by putting yourself in their shoes and trying to comprehend their point of view and emotions. Communicate truthfully with empathy.
5. If feasible, offer suggestions or propose substitutes to resolve the issue. A concrete strategy for improvement can make the truth more bearable, like a guiding light in the darkness.
6. Choose a safe and welcoming environment for questions and honest emotional expression. Be ready to engage in a conversation that promotes growth and understanding.
7. Avoid Blame: When sharing a hard truth, focus on the issue rather than blaming the person. It can reduce defensiveness and help them accept the facts.
8. Take responsibility for your actions and any influence you may have had if you were involved.

9. Be sincere and allow the person time to absorb the truth and its implications. Your patient will allow them the space to come to terms with their situation.

10. Remember that some truths are best left unspoken, especially if they will only inflict needless pain and serve no positive purpose. Consider the repercussions and think twice before disclosing a complicated truth to someone.

Further, it is essential to note the two concepts of truth: objective and subjective. Objective truth is independent of individual perspectives and beliefs (like the Bible). Meanwhile, subjective truth is a truth that is experienced or understood by an individual.

For example, statements like "1 + 2 = 3" are objective truth. However, comments like "vanilla ice cream is the best flavor" are subjective and dependent on preferences. So, subjectivism relies on subjective feelings, opinions, and interpretations instead of concrete facts. Instead of definite factuality, they predicated their option on emotional and personal concepts. Aesthetics and ethics are exceptional to individuals but lack universal acceptance. Subjective experiences, cultural background, and societal norms shape diverse opinions on aesthetic preferences.

However, objective truths (Sacred Scriptures) have withstood the test of time. The Bible is verifiable and universally applicable, using methods not dependent on humankind's bias or opinion. One can find an extensive compilation of scientific facts within the Holy Writ. Archaeologists have discovered the natural world's mathematical principles, historical events, and physical properties. Objective truth is foundational in many fields, including science, philosophy, and epistemology. It supports a shared understanding of the world and accurate decision-making.

Still, speaking the truth can be challenging or even risky. However, the truth is vital in many ethical and moral frameworks. Being honest and truthful promotes trust and open communication in personal and societal contexts. Yet, it can be tricky sometimes, and speaking the truth might be difficult or risky. Therefore, we should consider our intentions behind telling the truth. For instance, are we doing it to inform, educate, or help someone, or is it to hurt, harm, or create unnecessary conflict? If your intentions are righteous, it makes sense to speak the truth.

However, speaking the truth about hurting someone is unkind and harmful. Honesty and open communication build relationships. So, it is essential to consider the impact of your words on others. Sometimes, it may be necessary to address harsh truths. Prioritize compassion and respect, avoiding intentional emotional harm.

Truth can be complex and subjective. Therefore, it usually requires empathy, judgment, and a consideration of the potential outcomes. Different strategies may be necessary due to varying circumstances. For instance, the primary aim must be to balance honesty and compassion to minimize harm.

Jesus spoke, "He was the way and the truth and the life. No one comes to The Father except through Him" (John 14:6). Jesus is claiming to represent the ultimate truth or reality. Christ is The Author and Perfecter of Our Faith (Hebrews 12: 2). He embodies GOD's truth, wisdom, and Divine Nature in Christian theology. Christ, the Savior, is the Revelation of GOD's Character and the source of spiritual truth.

A fresh, Jesus' teachings are a moral and ethical truth guide. Most religions consider his words and actions a standard of truthfulness and righteousness. The Father's Son is a central figure in Christianity, and His teachings are the foundation of Christian ethics and morality. Despite interpretation differences, Jesus' teachings are consistent across Christian denominations and individuals.

The concept of Satan in Christianity symbolizes evil, deceit, and temptation. He is the ultimate deceiver and the embodiment of falsehood. In this context, He opposes the truth and works to obscure or distort it. The Bible regards Satan as a fallen angel who rebelled against GOD and cost him his place in heaven. Because of his rebellion, he is the epitome of deception, temptation, and evil.

So, in Satan's relationship with the truth, he is the "father of lies" and a deceiver. The Bible roots this concept of Lucifer as an outlier in various passages, most notably in the New Testament. In the Gospel of John, for example, Jesus calls Satan the "father of lies" and states there is no truth in him:

"You belong to your father, the devil, and you want to carry out your father's desires. He was a murderer from the beginning, not holding to the truth, for there is no truth in him. When he lies, he speaks his native language, for he is a liar and The Father of lies." (John 8: 44, NIV). The term "father of lies" emphasizes Satan's role in spreading untruths. The concept of misperception comes from Biblical passages depicting him as a deceiver and incarnation of evil.

Satan is the embodiment of deceit and the antithesis of truth. So, GOD and Jesus encouraged everybody to resist Satan's temptations and deception and to seek truth, righteousness, and the light of GOD. Despite the level of challenge, there is always a hint of brightness in every situation. If only we were bold enough to acknowledge it. If only we had the bravery to embrace it. So, when facing challenges, there is always a potential for positive outcomes and personal growth. But we must have the courage to seek the living truth of the Word.

James 4:7 encourages believers to resist the devil. When one fights, one opposes or strives against a particular entity or situation. Resistance is a defensive strategy that can fight or resist sin's allure. We can use the offensive weapon known as the sword of the Spirit, which represents the Word of GOD. The most effective means to resist and overcome Satan's lies and temptations is by utilizing the authenticity of the Scriptures.

GOD intended an interdependent versus interpreted within the entire text. When anybody verses out of context, it can lead to misinterpretations or misunderstandings of the intended meaning. The Passage emphasizes the need to submit to GOD. Then you can "Resist the devil, and he will flee from you" (James 4:7). To resist the devil, one must also submit to GOD. A disobedient or unsubmissive believer will not see victory.

Moral judgment wins favor, but the way of the unfaithful leads to their destruction. All who are prudent act with knowledge, but fools expose their folly. A wicked messenger falls into trouble, but a trustworthy envoy brings healing. Proverbs 13:15-17. Upholding truth and living it leads to a refined character. The virtue of faithfulness generates positive impressions that create opportunities for individuals.

The above principle applies to every sphere of life. It is a common challenge for individuals to avoid facing the truth about themselves. However, lying about nutritional habits, child neglect, or disregard for a spouse can ruin someone's reputation. Such faithlessness serves as a solid basis for the manifestation of duplicity.

A spiritual, evil realm constantly encircled us. Sometimes, we wonder if we could live differently. We might be more aware, in tune, and alert to the battles surrounding us and to the evil seeking to take control.

The enemy's schemes are ruthless and cunning. The Bible reminds us that his principal aim is to steal, kill, and destroy. If you are a child of the living King, never believe for a second that the enemy has not planned your demise. He will do everything he can to bring every believer down. That is his goal, and he will stop at nothing to accomplish it.

Christian truth refers to the core beliefs and teachings of Christianity, a monotheistic faith centered on Jesus Christ. So, Christian truth encompasses a range of theological and moral principles central to confidence in the Atoning Sacrifice for Our sins (1 John 2: 2).

Individual experiences, culture, and beliefs shape people's perspectives on Christianity or any religion. Despite criticism and controversies around the Christian faith, it has 2.38 billion followers. And by far is the largest religion by population, respectively. Christians find meaning, purpose, and community in their faith. An open dialogue helps address misunderstandings and promotes understanding.

Honesty and truthfulness are essential virtues in many ethical and moral systems, including Christianity. The Bible encourages Christians to be truthful for several reasons. One, no one is perfect. Two, Christians believe in the transformative power of repentance and forgiveness for those who seek a more honest life. Therefore, GOD's people must value compassion and forgiveness, even when others make mistakes.

CHAPTER 10

Individuals who experience a profound dread of men will inevitably encounter many difficulties in completing their essential responsibilities for GOD, as any action performed in GOD's name typically results in persecution.

Persecution

The writer was in Togo, the City of Lomé, Africa. He sat with pastors. They shared stories about other religions persecuting them. But one pastor shared a different story. He said that his ancestors passed it down for many generations. His story moved the writer so much that they felt it deserved a place in this chapter.

He tells how his people lived in a land where fear cast a long shadow over the hearts of its people. But a young girl named Lila lived in the village. She was bright-eyed and spirited. Her firm determination was surprising for her tender age. But in this world, where fitting in was paramount, Lila's rebellious spirit stood out like a sore thumb.

Persecution haunted her since birth. Her laughter echoed defiance, and her curiosity dared to question the status quo. The elders of the village, gripped by their insecurities, saw her as a harbinger of chaos.

As Lila grew, so did the hatred towards her. She faced rejection and condemnation from her peers, community, and those in power. Amidst the darkness, Lila found solace in her dreams' flickering light.

She often found solace on the village outskirts, embraced by the woods. Surrounded by ancient trees, she found belonging. In solitude, she found her true purpose.

In the evening, Lila found a hidden moonlit clearing. A solitary figure stood in the center. Shadows veiled him, but he exuded a comforting and wise presence.

He explained his ancestors did not know the Holy Spirit. So, she called him the Elder of the Woods, a guardian of ancient secrets and keeper of forgotten tales. The Elder's eyes sparkled like stars. They beckoned Lila, drawing her into a world beyond fear and prejudice.

Guided by the Elder, Lila discovered her dormant power. She found the strength in her voice, the courage in her heart, and the resilience of her spirit. She became a beacon of hope for those who lost their way by embracing her true self.

But, as Lila thrived in the woods, the shadow of persecution loomed closer. The village elders, threatened by her confidence, plotted to extinguish her ignited light.

On one fateful night, they descended upon the clearing. They had torches in hand. Malice and fear twisted their faces. Instead of resistance, they encountered Lila's gentle radiance.

At that moment, the villagers saw no threat but a reflection of their insecurities. The light of understanding cleared their hearts.

Lila's reputation shifted from outcast to guide and friend. Persecution scars served as a reminder of her inner strength and the light in dark times.

Her story shows when faced with persecution, The Father strengthens supporters. They endure tough times after they trust Him. The Bible reads: "The LORD himself goes before you and will be with you; He will never leave or forsake you. Do not be afraid of the world's punishment." Deuteronomy 31:8. The first book of the Bible is Genesis. The last book is Revelation. GOD reminds us not to fear them. 2 Timothy 1:7: "For GOD has not given us a Spirit of fear but of power and love and a sound mind."

Fear is a response to a perceived threat or danger. It is essential to human experience and helps people react to threats. We can also learn fear through experiences. For instance, someone with harmful expertise may develop a fear of it. An individual's direct or observational learning can lead to the development of fear. Thus, the transformation of fear has made it a critical survival tool. The response above encompasses the release of stress hormones, like adrenaline. They heighten heart rate, sharpen senses, and deliver a surge of energy.

The New Testament has many examples. Persecutors targeted Christians for believing in Christ. All the same, the world's discrimination is not a reason to fear. The Glorified anxiety has driven the worst parts of Church history. So, do not be afraid.

The writer has gone to many regions across the globe. In these places, Christians fear abuse because of their beliefs. However, responding to such abuse is subjective. When individuals trust Jesus, they will draw strength from their faith, not fear. Confidence is a potent source of drawing power. It changes how we face challenges. The resilient spirit turns to faith as a wellspring of strength.

So, a better word for fear is "androphobia." It means having an irrational or excessive fear of men. Androphobia is like many phobias. It can show itself in diverse ways. These include anxiety, panic, and avoidance. Overwhelming stress exceeds the actual threat level characterized by phobias. It is essential to tell an obsessive fear from a cautious fear.

Normal fear is of GOD. Righteous fearfulness promotes positive values, love, and compassion. It does not cause harm or persecution. Holy trepidation is crucial for human development. The fear of The LORD has helped us survive by promoting quick responses to Christian danger. Yet, with Christianity, there are a variety of interpretations, denominations, and individual beliefs. People's experiences with Christianity can differ. What one sees as a positive or negative aspect can vary.

Still, when fear is too much or irrational, it may become a phobia or anxiety disorder. These can harm the Saint's well-being more. Proverbs 9:10 states, "Respect for The LORD starts wisdom. To understand is to know the Holy One. In this context, the Fear of GOD is a foundation for a life lived by Divine principles.

But earthbound phobias often disrupt a believer's daily life and well-being. The above leads them to go to great lengths to avoid what they fear. Yet admitting mistakes and failures is critical. It is crucial for personal and professional growth. Failure is not the opposite of success but a part of the journey toward persecution. However, each failure can offer insights into what went wrong and how to improve. So, it is crucial to treat Christianity with care and respect. Beliefs and views can vary among individuals.

Church leaders should manage discussions about dangers to the Christian faith with care. They should avoid generalizations or misunderstandings. Yet, if someone has androphobia or another phobia, telling GOD about it can help. It can help deal with and control these fears.

Give all your anxieties to Him. He cares for you. (1 Peter 5:7). The Scripture carries a sense of deep concern, love, and attention. It is a reassuring sentiment to know someone cares for us. An open and warm connection provides comfort. It also encourages many parts of life.

Likewise, righteous fear is the fear of The LORD. Judeo-Christian traditions use it. The meaning has a deep reverence, awe, and respect for the Divine Almighty. Fear of Him is not terror or anxiety. The above is profound humility. Everything acknowledges His greatness, Holiness, and authority. They refer to the infinite qualities of righteousness. It also refers to Jesus Christ's Omnipotence. Then, it relates to transcendence beyond the limits of the material world. But it also implies a supreme and unparalleled size that surpasses human understanding.

However, distinct cultures, religions, and personal backgrounds lead to varying beliefs. They lead to beliefs about persecution and fear. Nontrinitarianism may reveal resilience in the community. It can show inner strength or external support. But the Glorified relies on Jesus Christ. This reliance goes beyond nature. For Christians, Christ is the Son of the Supreme Being and is SOMEONE to rely on beyond the natural dominion. "The natural kingdom only gives birth to natural things. But the spiritual kingdom births supernatural life." John 3:6.

For instance, In Acts 10:38, Paul says, "GOD anointed Jesus of Nazareth with the Holy Spirit and power. He did good, healing people oppressed by the devil, for The Father was with him. The LORD did excellent work. So, the Pharisees hated Jesus. The Pharisaic Demigods did not like his success with the Jews. These religious leaders were envious of His ministry. Thus, they persecuted the Author of Salvation (Hebrews 2:10) because of His good works. GOD's people challenge social norms and advocate for righteous change. They may face resistance or persecution. It comes from those who feel threatened by the proposed changes.

The Bible contains many passages about enduring pain for the sake of Christ. During the New Testament era, Jesus' followers faced social isolation. The religious leaders heralded harsh persecution of them (Acts 4:1–3). But Jesus taught, "He will bless those persecuted for being right. They will receive the kingdom of heaven" (Matthew 5:10). Righteousness is a deep connection with GOD's power. It brings peace and joy that goes beyond outside circumstances. This inner well-being is resilient in life's challenges. It stems from faith in the material and temporal aspects of existence.

The Author of Life reminded His disciples that the world hated and persecuted Him first (John 15:18). Yet, He will bless those persecuted for being right. They will get the kingdom of heaven" (Matthew 5:10).

In this verse, Jesus is talking to His disciples. He is preparing them to face the challenges they might encounter because of their association with him. He tells them the world's hate is predictable since it also despises him.

Thousands of people suffer daily for Christ's sake and are thankful. So, "Everyone who wants to live in Christ Jesus, the world will persecute them." Still, Jesus speaking to His supporters, "Start your cross and follow Him." Matthew 16:24-26.

In Jesus' day, the cross always symbolizes death. When a man carried a cross, they had condemned him to die on it. In the Savior's case, we see it as a symbol of Him being unfairly judged or burdened with heavy punishment. But He was innocent. But, for Christians today, it also shows embracing their duties. It shows their endurance and willingness to sacrifice to follow Jesus and live out their faith.

Still, the Scripture shows Jesus' ministry powers continue during challenging seasons. When Jesus' supporters face disappointment, the Bible teaches us. "All things work for our good" (Romans 8:28). It is why Paul saw his "tests" as chances for spiritual growth. Problems were subjective to him. They were a unique natural wonder, like the Grand Canyon or the Northern Lights. So, the Apostle rejoices in his weaknesses. He knows they invite Christ's power into him. (II Corinthians 12:9).

As the Saints embrace their weaknesses and rely on GOD's grace, it can lead to spiritual strength. Therefore, acknowledging personal weaknesses becomes an opportunity for Divine power to manifest. It suggests finding stability and growth by accepting and understanding human limits. Also, it means using challenges as a chance for personal growth and resilience.

Yet when this modern age encounters difficulties, they often wonder, WHY? Like Paul, we choose to trust GOD and accept His grace. We, too, will glory in trials. "We know that trial makes patience. And patience makes the experience. And experience makes hope. Hope makes us not ashamed. The Holy Ghost gives us hope by spreading the love of GOD in our hearts" (Romans 5:3–5). This verse is part of a more significant Passage. The Apostle Paul discusses how being right with GOD benefits believers. Accuracy and morality happen through faith in Jesus Christ.

GOD wants His children to learn the discipline of seeking answers through Him. And perceive challenging situations as growth opportunities. (1 Corinthians 2:14, Romans 8:16–17). At that moment of trust, He confirms your relationship with Him, comforts you, and leads you into all truth. We then feel a deep connection with The Hope of Glory. He is the King Eternal (1 Timothy 1:17). He provides comfort and guidance.

The Holy Spirit begins the supernatural work of transforming us through problems. GOD uses the tests and trials to develop our character and ministry as we mature in our faith. But the Atoning Sacrifice helps believers endure trials. It also leads to the development of positive qualities. My dear ones, do not find it odd when you encounter fiery difficulties. Instead, be glad because you are sharing in the sufferings of Christ. But bitterness is inevitable. It is true unless a believer embraces GOD's grace to deal with anguish. Rely on GOD in challenging times. Dark moments can help you avoid resentment and grow closer to GOD's grace and awareness. (James 1:2-3).

Your ability to find gratitude in challenging situations requires deep faith. Scripture commands believers to express gratitude always (I Thessalonians 5:18). Choosing gratitude over complaints means suppressing natural urges. Psalm 107:22 refers to this choice as a sacrifice of thanksgiving. Along with giving thanks, The LORD tells us to rejoice in everything. "Rejoice in The LORD always" (Philippians 4:4). Thanking GOD requires a choice. Rejoicing is a soul's spontaneous reaction.

The size of His Holy power is far beyond any pain we may undergo. Although suffering can be brutal, it is not without purpose. The Creator uses certain circumstances to teach powerful lessons. Or to achieve His

Divine plan. For instance, suffering can help you grow. It can aid in spiritual development or be part of GOD's plan. It motivates followers to find meaning in their suffering. They must trust GOD's wisdom and purpose, even during tough times.

Jehovah values our faith more than precious metal. Trials are a chance for joy. We know they evaluate our faith and build steadfastness. Yet, the Saints must allow perseverance to have its full effect so we may be complete and lacking in nothing. (James 1:4). So, trials make us strong. The LORD will enable trials in our lives. But, even when things are bleak, it works for our good and GOD's glory. (Romans 8:28).

Still, our human mindset cannot understand the purpose. Jehovah Jireh permits us to encounter the trial. For instance, if The Hope of Glory challenges us as the Author and Perfecter of Our Faith. Hence, most mature Saints believe The Father wants us to execute His Intentions. Followers of "GOD's intentions" mean living by his teachings and principles. Believers think the will of the Blessed and Only Ruler is (1 Timothy 6:15). Righteousness involves acts of faith, worship, moral living, and service to others.

Also, developed Christians understand GOD exercises His sovereignty over pain and suffering. Most young people the writer counseled claim this. They say interpreting the Bible does not relate to their lives or problems. So, these baby Saints fall away from the faith and leave the Church after their peace goes awry. Then, they usually find info that challenges their beliefs on the internet and in science.

Inexperienced believers may find reconciling specific scientific findings with Christian teachings difficult. So, they turn to social media. Social media can confuse young people with conflicting views about the Bible. The theory of evolution and the affirmation of nonheterosexuality goes against Biblical tenets. So, when problems arise, the web's immoral teachings offer no solutions. Unethical behavior does not contribute to finding constructive solutions.

Those who adhere to non-Christian religious teachings must grasp the unfavorable outcomes. Yet secular organizations, therapists, and community groups specialize in supporting individuals. They help people through different life challenges. These resources can help people who do not rely on Christian teachings to solve problems. They can be valuable.

However, the writer believes that GOD's way is better. Jehovah knows everything and has a good plan for our lives. He is Holy and tells us what is right and wrong and wants us to follow His commands. We will experience His peace and joy when we trust and obey His Word. The Bible encourages followers to stick to righteous moral and ethical principles. Inner virtues are for a harmonious and fulfilling life. The Word provides a shared framework. It helps Christians handle challenges and decide as a group.

Also, in times of distress, GOD offers unmatched comfort to believers (Psalm 34:18). The agony on this planet is transient, as He has pledged to eradicate every tear from our eyes (Revelation 21:4). Amid our suffering, He transforms malevolent intentions into positive outcomes (Genesis 50:20).

GOD's Love is beyond human understanding. Our finite nature limits us by the constraints of our physical and mental abilities. Thus, ideas like infinity and eternity are hard to fathom. They go beyond our experience. The same goes for Divine love. However, we know it is valid through Biblical history and secular text. We also know it through our convictions. Humans can only understand GOD's Love at a minimum. But even from the smallest amount, His love leads us to trust His guidance in tough times.

Again, the human intellect is incapable of grasping the concept of GOD. Our knowledge is incomplete in defining Jehovah. We cannot recount who Jehovah is. He "dwells in unapproachable light" (1 Timothy 6:16). If the Almighty is incomprehensible, so is his love. But Jesus teaches His disciples about love. "From a human standpoint, this is impossible." However, not with the Creator. "Everything is possible." (Matthew 19:26).

It is challenging to make sense of a troubling incident and what comes after. Thus, the journey toward healing can seem like an impossible task. Once more, "With man, this is impossible, but with GOD, all things are possible." So, when facing challenges, pray and submit to the True Vine (John 15:1). This will improve emotional and physical healing. The LORD's people have overcome unimaginable deeds in the Bible. His rules are not demanding for the righteous. Jesus takes accountability for them. We cannot meet the Almighty's demands. Yet, His Son's sacrificial death carries the weight for us.

Still, everyone will experience grim times that can bring sadness, anxiety, and stress. But building resilience in Jesus Christ will help the Saint. It will support a positive outlook during the struggle. Jesus, The Author of Life (Acts 3:15), empowers us to face an unclear future with courage. We can overcome even the most challenging times. The verse is a proclamation about Jesus.

Peter's idea is about empowerment and courage in life's challenges. It draws strength from the belief in Jesus as a source of authority. It aligns with Christian teachings. They are about finding resilience through faith in Jesus Christ. Righteous conviction is genuine, even in uncertain times. Trust provides believers with comfort, guidance, and courage in life's challenges.

To quote Ray A. Davis: "A challenge only becomes an obstacle when you bow to it."

CHAPTER 11

It is up to Christians to decide if they want to make happiness their prevailing state of mind. We will observe our world's remarkable transformation if we dedicate our internal dialog to righteous contentment daily.

Self-talk

Everybody knew the writer for his gentle demeanor and warm smile. But, under his cheerfulness lay a tangled web of self-doubt and insecurity.

Inside his mind, self-talk filled Jocephus' days. It was a continuous, soft murmur. These whispers were encouraging. They uplifted his spirits and guided him through life's challenges. But they were more often misleading. They planted seeds of doubt and fear. The seeds took root deep in his soul.

Jocephus strolled through Forest Park in St. Louis, Missouri, one fateful morning. He overheard the ladies ahead of him. They felt excited. They were attending a workshop on the power of positive thinking. It promised to change lives through the magic of self-talk. Intrigued, the writer attended, hoping to quiet the storm within his mind.

A charismatic speaker led the workshop. He preached the gospel of self-affirmation and confidence. Jocephus listened. He hung on every word as the man extolled the value of self-belief. By the end of the session, he felt a glimmer of hope flicker within his heart.

Eager to use his new knowledge, Jocephus repeated affirmations each morning. He told himself he was worthy, capable, and deserving of success. At first, it seemed to work wonders. His confidence soared, and he tackled challenges with newfound determination.

But as days turned into weeks, Jocephus' self-talk took a darker turn. The whispers once lifted his spirits. Now, they were mocking his every move. They remind him of past failures and shortcomings. No matter how hard he tried to silence them, they grew louder and more relentless with each passing day.

He feared he was losing his grip on reality. The writer sought solace in the quietness of prayer. He hoped to find peace amidst the towering voice and babbling self-talk. But even during prayer, he let his mind wander. The voices followed him, taunting him with endless chatter.

Jocephus confided in the wise Holy Spirit. The Spirit dwelled deep within his heart. The writer was desperate for respite. With a knowing voice, the Spirit beckoned him closer. It whispered words of wisdom that resonated deep within his soul.

GOD's Words were encouraging. "Dear child," "The biggest danger is not in the words we speak to others, but in the ones we whisper to ourselves. For they can shape our reality, for better or worse."

At that moment, Jocephus realized the genuine danger of self-talk. It was not just about positive thinking or self-affirmation. It was about growing compassion and kindness towards oneself. With new clarity, he vowed to silence the voices of doubt. Instead, he would embrace the gentle whispers of self-love.

He emerged from prayer. The golden light of Holiness bathed him. Jocephus felt a weight lift from his shoulders. The journey to self-acceptance would be long and hard. But he knew he was no longer alone. With each step he took, he whispered words of encouragement. He knew that true strength lay not in silencing the voices but in learning to listen to the Holy Spirit.

Negative self-talk stems from internal and external factors. For example, if someone faces criticism, rejection, or unrealistic expectations. They come from parents, caregivers, or peers. Aimless wandering could have happened during childhood. Traumatic experiences or a lack of positive reinforcement can affect negative self-perception.

Also, the society and culture in which a person grows up could affect their self-talk. People may take in destructive beliefs if the culture values perfectionism, competition, or unrealistic standards.

Constructive messages individuals tell themselves refer to good self-talk. For instance:

- "I believe in myself and my GOD-given abilities."
- "I can overcome challenges in Jesus' Name."
- "I trust in my decision-making skills to Christ."

A bright outlook on the Word shapes one's mindset, emotions, and well-being. Positive self-talk can boost confidence, motivation, and resilience. Negative self-talk can fuel self-doubt, raise stress, and lower self-esteem.

The internal dialogue or monologue humans have with themselves is self-talk. It relates to the messages people tell themselves. One's inner thoughts can affect one's emotions, behavior, and mental well-being. The thoughts can be positive, negative, or neutral.

Everyone, including Christians, has tough times. These times cause negative self-talk from depression, low confidence, and anxiety. The clarification escapes the Glorified and explains why the struggle is happening. Often, in tough seasons, it seems the Saints have no power. They cannot control adversity. But GOD did not give us a Spirit of timidity, but a Spirit of power, love, and self-discipline — 2 Timothy 1:7.

However, when we expect the worst, it creates a belief that life will not improve. It makes us feel empty. But we do not know why.

But positive, righteous self-talk has helpful messages. They boost confidence, motivation, and resilience. Yet, negative self-talk can present itself in a multitude of ways. Below are five examples:

1. "I lack skill in my goal. So, I should not attempt it to stay safe."
2. "I'm failing and can't seem to get anything right."
3. "I do not have the right to experience happiness."
4. "I will fail, regardless of my efforts. What is the purpose of even attempting?"
5. "It looks hard. So, even if I tried, I could never do it."

After the Glorified accepts the lies of the above bullet points as Gospel truth, they can no longer see themselves as someone worth living. Then, they blame others or themselves. Self-pity strains their relationships and hinders their personal growth. The individual boastfulness about themselves is self-centeredness. They believe they need not improve because nothing is wrong with them. These are the pessimistic, egoistical self-talk that impedes personal development.

Usually, when we reach arrogance, a small voice in our mind turns negative. Failing to heed signs from the Holy Spirit raises the likelihood of going astray. It makes life hard. Denial thinking convinces us we will forever be out of reach of our dreams or unable to fulfill our goals.

Then, a Saint becomes content with elementary things in life. Delve into your Christian values, goals, and aspirations. It is essential to plan to achieve them. Remember that it is never too late to move from condemning to succeeding. Besides, Romans 8:34-38 tells us:

"Who has the power to condemn? No one (us inclusive). Christ Jesus, Who died—more than that, Who GOD raised to life—is at the right hand of GOD and is also interceding for us. Who will separate us from the love of Christ? Will trouble, hardship, persecution, famine, nakedness, danger, or sword? The Word tells us: For your sake, we face death all day long, and the world considers us as sheep for the slaughter pen. No, in all these things, we are more than conquerors through Him who loved us. I am convinced that nothing can separate us from His love. Not death or life, not angels or demons, not the present or the future, and no powers."

The Apostle Paul reminds us about criticizing ourselves. It cannot boost self-awareness or efficiency. Unwise criticism is not helpful. So, the Saints must ensure it does not harm. If we are not careful, it also creates significant stress for us and those around us. Negative self-talk is an inner dialogue with yourself. It may limit your ability to believe in yourself and your skills and reach your goals. Thoughts that lessen your ability to improve your life should be silent.

The Apostle Paul tells us in Philippians 4:8 to think about these things: What is authentic, Holy, upright, and pure? The writer believes Christians have control over our thoughts. When negative random thoughts pop into our conscious, we can replace them with Holy ones.

Deep inside, we have an innate inclination to critique and evaluate GOD's Exalted. The nature of Adam, before his fall, was pure and untainted by sin. The attributes he had were unlike any other found. Romans 5:12 highlights that the sinful acquisition resulted from Adam's fall.

The amalgamation of human and GOD's Character now lived within him. In this context, a better term for [nature] might be [capacity]. In the fall, Adam gained a capacity for sin, which changed his heart. But, upon embracing Christianity, people gain a new ability. They can connect with and understand GOD.

Negative self-talk results from internal and external factors contributing to its development. For example, if someone faces criticism. They might also face rejection or unrealistic expectations from parents, caregivers, or peers. Again, this could have happened during childhood.

Traumatic experiences or a lack of positive reinforcement can affect negative self-perception.

Also, the society and culture in which a person grows up can affect their self-talk. People may take in destructive beliefs if the culture values perfectionism or unrealistic standards. Negative chatter will drown out any positive meaning. Ambiguous discouragement will cause harmful feelings.

Within every person lies an internal worldly nature, ready to pass judgment. Sometimes, this inner chatterbox is audible, like a gentle whisper in the wind. Other times, it is loud because of anxiety or stress. Still, our negative inner monologue enjoys influencing us. It pushes us to keep old beliefs and dwell on past regrets and missed chances.

So, at the GOD-forsaken hour of 3 a.m., the critical inner voice becomes our unwelcome alarm. Doubts creep into our minds. They plant seeds of self-doubt and make us question our worth and accomplishments.

Saints, please understand the power of negative self-talk and inner hostility. It judges us and goes beyond our personal lives. Then, we compare ourselves to those around us. When we do not measure up, it makes us feel less competent and deserving. That is why the Apostle wrote: Ephesians 4:29 states, "Do not say bad things. Say what builds others up to help them; that may benefit those who listen."

The Bible has many examples of Christians' challenges. They faced adversity and beat it with faith and prayer. In Esther's book, she and her uncle, Mordecai, face life-threatening situations. But they never give in to negative self-talk. Instead, they turn the problem around through prayer and fasting. In the New Testament, Jesus did many miracles. He healed the sick and fed the hungry. These miracles showed his power over tough times.

That said, Christians do not have power over all adverse circumstances. Yet, they control the thoughts they choose. They can find strength and comfort through faith and prayer in demanding times. "I have told you these things, so that in me you may have peace. In this world, you will have trouble. But take heart! I have overcome the world" (John 16:33). The Apostle Peter writes, "Cast all your (challenges) anxiety on The LORD because He cares for us." (1 Peter 5:7).

So, criticizing oneself through self-talk makes no one feel better. It leads to more negative thoughts that trigger stress and anxiety. Constant worrying can contribute to ongoing tension and uneasiness. Carnal supporters, especially, are hard on themselves. If you have persistent negative thoughts or emotions, you must contact friends, family, or a mental health pro. They can offer the support and guidance you need.

Nonbelievers focus on success. They do not share their beliefs but fear failure. They struggle to balance faith and worldly matters with The LORD. These skeptics do not adhere to a particular religious belief. They can have diverse views on life, purpose, and success. For instance, some may focus on personal achievements, career goals, or societal contributions. Others may rank relationships or self-improvement. They seek a fulfilling life without the Supreme Being.

But Christians rely on (THE FIRSTBORN OVER ALL CREATION) (Colossians 1:15) during a struggle. The Holy Writ backs the principle. Supporters find true happiness in Christ through self-talk. It inspires them to submit to Him out of a deep desire. We, as believers, must depend on the Great High Priest (Hebrews 4:14). We need him for our redemption, leadership, mercy, and daily needs. Faith in GOD brings satisfaction and turns life's struggles into meaningful works.

However, focusing inward through self-deprecation hinders our relationship with Jesus Christ. The Psalmist writes Chapter 9:9-10, "The LORD is a shelter for the oppressed, a refuge in times of trouble. Those who know Your name trust in You, for You, O LORD, do not abandon those who seek You." So, we must have unwavering confidence in THE AUTHOR of LIFE. It must surpass our fleeting emotions and experiences during adversity. Thus, faith means believing GOD can help us, even if we do not understand it.

Still, Satan would have us believe that our sin is so burdensome that we cannot confront the Savior. However, we must not allow our genuine sense of conflict to consume us. The struggle should cause us to turn to the only One Who can oversee them. He is the Author and Perfecter of Our Faith (see Hebrew. 12:2). It means requesting Jesus to absolve us of our "struggle" and serve as our Savior (John 3:16). We need only to commit to following Jesus since He is both GOD and man, and He created and saved the world. His Holy Spirit transforms us from the inside out and enables us to serve and obey Him.

Self-criticism is more brutal than criticism from others. Self-criticism is the conversation within our mind. It is the thing we say to ourselves when alone. Our inner voice engulfs us during moments of idleness and work commutes. Or after heated conversations, social media consumption, and navigating stressful traffic.

But, by telling The Advocate (1 John 2:1) about our mental turmoil, we can find the ties that cause the most pain. The cause of our misery stems from the physical branches we cling to apart from Christ. As our world walks through these unique times, we should challenge ourselves to cling to The LORD. You will fear The LORD your GOD, serve and cling to Him, and swear by HIS NAME (Deuteronomy 10:20).

An individual is the most influential person in their heart. So, the content of their self-talk is significant. Outside factors can influence thoughts and feelings. Afresh, believers have the power to accept or reject unproductive thoughts. For instance, the Saints can create righteous boundaries to change their struggling mindset. Turning to GOD during tough times helps us cope and recover.

But we must never forget this because of Jesus Christ's atonement. He takes our pains, sicknesses, temptations, and afflictions. So, we can manipulate our reactions to the struggle. Thus, how believers react during the storm may make stress worse. Or it may lead to their problem-solving. Hence, overcoming obstacles can contribute to our advancement.

Self-talk is a significant hindrance to overcoming a challenging time. It is how we talk to ourselves. Our internal dialogue can offer encouragement and inspiration and boost our self-esteem. But Lucifer's influencing our inner voice. He is speaking into our Spirit. It tells us we have the power to:

a. Shake off troubles
b. You can feel better
c. You do not need Jesus

Then pride fueled your story. Unwanted thoughts can ruin Holy experiences and distract from significance value, draining energy. Struggles can also make you feel anxious and depressed. Fortunately, you can replace negative thinking with righteous thoughts. You can do this by appealing to The Hope of Glory. Paul writes in Romans 5:3-5, "We can glory in our sufferings. They make us persevere and build character and hope."

If you find your mind is still gravitating towards failure, focus on the thoughts in your mind. Think and pray before responding to negative self-talk. Then, decide if your thoughts are helpful or harmful. Pay close attention to The Righteous Counsel. They explain how to shift your self-talk to be affirmative. The writer of Proverbs 19:20-21, "There are many devices in a man's heart but the counsel of The LORD, which must stand."

Unwanted thoughts can ruin Holy experiences, distract from important things, and drain energy. They can also make you feel anxious and depressed by aiming for The Hope of Glory. You can replace corrupt thoughts with good ones. Do not focus on the negativity. Think about the positive and the people who want you to succeed. It benefits both parties involved.

Note the self-defeating communications playing on a loop in your mind. Think and pray before responding to these thoughts. Then, decide if the conceptions are helpful or harmful. Be attentive to the counsel of the Holy Spirit on how to change your self-talk to Holy Linguistics.

Try replacing negative self-talk with positive affirmations to reduce stress and boost self-esteem. Monitor your thoughts and identify any negative self-talk that may hold you back. Our bodies are unique and deserve love and care. The LORD created us in his likeness. We have the Triad's worth and abilities. GOD's Love is crucial for human well-being.

Saints overcome challenges by acknowledging Jesus' power. Yet, they must keep reminding themselves. Problems do not show their virtuous nature. With Jesus Christ's help, they can rise above adversities.

It is best if you go from condemning thoughts to succeeding. To take an official stand of righteousness requires self-reflection. It would help if you built a positive mindset in the Word. You must set goals and act toward them. Remember that the journey from negative self-talk may take time. Be patient and stay committed to the positive changes you make in your mindset and actions.

It is challenging to conquer negative self-talk. However, a positive mindset is crucial for well-being. Here are strategies that may help:

1. Consciousness: Pay attention to your thoughts. Recognize when negative self-talk happens and its patterns. Challenge the accuracy of your negative thoughts. Determine if they are facts or assumptions.
2. Be kind to yourself. Show yourself the kindness and understanding you would give a friend. They are dealing with similar challenges. Mistakes and setbacks are part of everyone's journey. Practice self-care during tough times.

3. Encouraging words: Offset negative thoughts by using righteous affirmations. Substitute negative self-statements with positive and empowering alternatives. Practice these affirmations for a positive mindset.

4. Cognitive restructuring: Challenge negative thoughts. Replace irrational thoughts with realistic ones. Open your mind to different perspectives and see the positive side of things.

5. Gratitude exercise: Focus on the positives in your life. Be grateful for the things you appreciate. Keep a gratitude journal to shift your focus from negativity.

6. Surround yourself with positive energy: Encircle yourself with supportive and positive people. Encouragement can combat negative self-talk. Avoid negative influences, including people, media, and environments.

7. Start small: Break big goals into smaller, reachable steps. Celebrate your successes along the way. Accept that perfection is unachievable and mistakes or challenges are acceptable.

Again, remember it takes time and effort to change thought patterns. So, be patient with yourself and celebrate the insignificant victories you experience. A second time, you can get professional help. It offers extra support and strategies tailored for persistent negative self-talk.

Finally, prayer can give structured time for self-reflection. It lets people think about their actions, feelings, and beliefs. It will let the Glorified express their emotions. They can share concerns and desires that are meaningful. Prayer can be a cathartic and therapeutic process to drown out negative self-talk. The writer uses prayer to seek guidance, clarity, and purpose. However, talking to GOD helps him reach his goals. It keeps his self-criticism in check.

CHAPTER 12

The journey toward building emotional and mental resilience and perseverance involves facing and surpassing many obstacles and challenges.

Rising Above Adversities

C hristians can rise above adversity. But they need a righteous heart. This heart needs resilience, determination, and a righteous mindset. It allows the Saints to view setbacks as temporary and solvable. Philippians 3:14 encourages believers to press on toward the goal. They do it for the prize of the upward call of GOD in Christ Jesus. In Christianity, resilience means trusting in GOD's plan. Endurance is steadfast even in tough times. It also means relying on faith to beat challenges.

For instance, in Jackson, Mississippi, a young boy named Julius lived in a rural area on College Street. He was a neighbor and friend of Jocephus. He was small in stature. But we all knew him for his calm spirit and unwavering faith in Jesus. Despite age eight, Julius faced adversaries that seemed impossible to many of us.

Julius grew up in a humble family. He often saw his parents struggle to make ends meet. His handyperson father worked hard to provide for their needs. His mother tended to their home with grace and love. Despite their hardships, their home was always a welcoming and warm place to hang out. We laughed, and they shared the warmth of their faith.

As Julius grew older, he met bullies. They mocked his beliefs and ridiculed his values. They taunted him for his kindness and labeled him as weak. But Julius stayed strong. He found strength in his prayers and the teachings of Jesus Christ.

One day, Julius walked home from school. He stumbled upon a group of children surrounding a frail, older man. They jeered at him, throwing insults and pushing him around. Without hesitation, Julius stepped forward, shielding the man with his own body.

"Why do you bother with him, Julius?" Sneered one bully. "He's a burden to society."

Julius looked at the man with compassion in his eyes. "Every life is precious in the eyes of Jesus," he spoke in soft tones. Julius stood his ground, gathering his courage, refusing to back down in the face of adversity.

Moved by Julius' bravery, the other children reconsidered their actions. They dropped their stones. Then they walked away, leaving Julius and the older adult alone on the rocky Emerson Road.

Tears welled in the older man's eyes as he grasped Julius' hand in gratitude. "Thank you, young man." "You have shown me kindness when others turned their backs."

With a vast smile, Julius' heart filled with joy. "It is the love of Jesus that guides me."

From that day on, Julius' courage spread through our rural community. It spread like wildfire. People spoke of his unwavering faith and willingness to stand for what was right. His enemies became allies. Julius became a beacon of hope for those facing oppression and injustice.

Years passed, and Julius' reputation as a man of faith only grew stronger. He continued to face challenges and obstacles on his journey. But, through it all, he kept believing he could overcome anything with Jesus.

Julius' story showed the power of faith. It also showed the triumph of love over adversity. It was all in the Name of Jesus.

That said, in Christ, He gives us the ability to bounce back from challenges. We can manage stress, recover from setbacks, and adapt to adversity. We can also maintain mental and emotional well-being during challenging times. Christians have faith in the Supreme Being. They trust in the Almighty. This faith and trust are their sources of strength and resilience. Believing in GOD's plan will bring comfort and purpose. Faith is notably true during tough times. The Creator's plan gives meaning to life's events. They are hard to understand now. Yet, he can give people meaning. He can help them find purpose in their experiences.

The ability to last in tough times lets people see problems are part of a larger Divine plan. It leads them to find meaning and hope in their experiences. This trust can add to resilience. It provides a base for coping with life's uncertainties. Yet, many factors can influence resilience. These factors include personal traits and social support. However, faith and trust in GOD's plan can offer stability. He will bolster your righteous strength, self-awareness, and intentional, prayerful life.

Also, Romans 12:2 emphasizes changing the mind. The message is: "Do not copy this world's pattern but change yourself by renewing your mind. Then, you can evaluate and approve GOD's good, pleasing, and perfect will. Psalm 30:5 also acknowledges suffering's brevity; "His anger lasts a moment, but his favor, a lifetime." Weeping may stay for the night, but rejoicing comes in the morning."

Christians who face challenges can find comfort in righteousness. It means using Biblical teachings to build resilience, determination, and a righteous mindset. The foundation provides Sacred support and Holy resources. They help believers see setbacks as temporary challenges they can conquer. It fosters a powerful belief in GOD's plan for their lives.

For example, various Bible verses encourage believers to be resilient in adversity. James 1:12 states, "Blessed is the one who persists under trial. They have passed the test. They will get the crown of life that The LORD promised to those who love Him. This verse encourages believers to have faith and endure challenges. We can overcome trials with steadfastness and faith. Hence, they will bring spiritual rewards. The "Crown of life" means not fearing what you will suffer for The LORD.

Dieter F. Uchtdorf analyzed it well: "It is your reaction to adversity, not the adversity itself, that determines how your life story will develop."

The Glorified must understand that facing adversity is natural. Our ability to bounce back is crucial for overcoming challenges and emerging stronger. So, we practice Holiness to mute negativism and to stay present and focused. It helps prevent emotions from being overwhelmed. Also, it allows the Saints to tackle one challenge at a time.

So, as the Saints link Holiness to reasonable beliefs, it can help shift their mind from negativity. It directs one's focus toward the Sacred and will promote a more Christ-like viewpoint.

A fuller take on "Rising Above Adversities" shows the resilient and transformative process. It is about overcoming tough challenges and distressing circumstances. The title of the author's book suggests overcoming obstacles. It means rising above them with strength, perseverance, and a growth-focused mindset. Believers with a "Courageous Spirit" understand a challenge as an opportunity to gain experience and grow. The righteous do not avoid difficulties. They approach them with a cheerful outlook. GOD sees setbacks as natural in learning.

A risen Christian must navigate hardships with grace and wisdom. They must also have a firm commitment to growth. It mirrors the journey of a Saint. Despite facing trials, the Saint ascends to a higher state of being. Righteous perseverance and determination will overcome any suggested hardships. Yet, we note that a positive mindset and determination are valuable. However, to overcome challenges, we must consider a mix of factors. These include practical strategies, adaptability, support, and faith.

To have a mindset of Holiness and perseverance, one must stay true to one's principles. They must also remain true to their values and ethics. Moral principles are necessary when navigating difficulties. Sanctitude involves not compromising on moral integrity, even in the face of adversity. The nobility of Spirit helps people navigate challenging situations with GOD's strength and conviction. It fosters a sense of purpose and dignity.

Which includes:

1. Whether it is a minor health issue or a medical emergency, we must seek The Advocate (1 John 2:1). GOD's help is dependable.
2. Financial troubles can arise without notice. But the Bread of Life (John 6:35) gives no room for supporters to worry about money. Valuables mean promises and conditions for those who follow Jesus (Matthew 6:33).
3. When relationships hit a rough patch, it can feel like walking on eggshells. Rather than being angry, the Mediator of the New Covenant (Hebrew 9:15) tells us to show them compassion. (1 John 4:20).
4. Coping with the death of a loved one is one of life's most tough challenges (Psalm 147:3). Grieving is a complex journey. It is crucial to show self-compassion as you go through it.
5. Professional or academic setbacks (James 1:2-4). Yet, setbacks are a part of life. We build resilience by overcoming them. So,

use setbacks as steppingstones for personal and professional growth.

Trusting in Jesus Christ's power is crucial for a Saint's success. It helps them rise above adversities. The long-suffer maintains a cheerful outlook regardless of the circumstances. They also know it is about learning from tough times and getting stronger. Emmanuel's supporters can beat obstacles by trusting The LORD. They must be tough, seek help from friends, and focus on His goodness. It is about finding the strength in The LORD to keep going and not give up, disregarding one's number of years.

Besides, 2 Corinthians 12:9—"My grace is all you need, for my power is the greatest when you are weak." Psalm 73:26—"My flesh and my heart may fail, but GOD is the strength of my heart and my portion forever." Nehemiah 8:10—"Do not grieve, for the joy of The LORD is your strength."

However, problems and concerns vary among individuals of different age groups. Stage of life, health, socioeconomic status, cultural background, and personal history shape adults. Toddlers and teenagers may face challenges. These include learning, socializing, self-discovery, and family dynamics. That is true. Young people face academic pressure, peer relationships, and self-discovery like anyone else.

Everyone is unique, and what works for one person may not work for another. A supportive and understanding environment is crucial. It helps young people navigate these challenges and become stronger and more resilient. Adolescents must feel that their experiences, emotions, and perspectives are valid. A supportive environment acknowledges their feelings. It allows them to express themselves without judgment.

To illustrate, fresh out of high school in St. Louis, Missouri, the writer took a job working in a steel mill. He sat around a table for lunch with men much older than he. They took turns sharing how they overcame adversity. They admitted overcoming hardship can be a challenging but transformative process. His coworkers were all older men. They talked about some strategies to help people navigate and overcome adversity.

1. Focus on solutions instead of dwelling on problems to maintain a positive mindset.
2. Contact trusted individuals and share your thoughts and feelings.
3. Embrace change and be adaptable.
4. Accept that adversity and change are inevitable in life.
5. Consider the lessons learned from challenging experiences.
6. Show yourself compassion.
7. Practice self-kindness and understanding.

But these men winked and smiled at the writer. By making light of it, they wanted to show that they were having fun and knew the writer was young. Their scenario suggests lighthearted, flirtatious interaction. The individuals involved make the author the center of their shared fun. They said,

"Jocephus, you haven't been through enough to understand life's twists and turns." After hearing their statement, the writer sat in silence. He recalled the hurt he still carried from not forgiving two older white men. His hatred began when he was twelve years old in Jackson, Mississippi. Unforgiveness was hurting him a lot. It harmed his mind, heart, and body. He was hiding behind a fake smile at them when all he wanted to do was hide and die.

Unforgiveness was perpetuating a cycle of hurt and conflict. Because he refused to forgive, Joecephus was contributing to ongoing disputes. He created a hostile environment for himself and others. Unforgiveness had clouded judgment to influence decision-making. So, holding onto resentment causes him to make emotional choices rather than rational ones, leading to sour outcomes.

Note the writer never talked with them about his story. At twelve, he rode his bike in Jackson, Mississippi, in the wrong neighborhood. After the older men exchanged racial slurs at him, they got into their car and chased him. They honked their horns, calling him the ("N" word), and ran him over. They left him lying in the streets, struggling to breathe and drained, fighting for life.

Unforgiveness overwhelmed him for many years. It caused him to hold on to resentment and anger. They were tiring and hurt the writer's well-being. It is essential to acknowledge these emotions and consider ways to address them.

Years later, my supervisor was another white man. He started sharing the Word of GOD with me about unforgiveness. After hearing my testimony, he shared Scriptures about forgiveness. He clarified that forgiveness does not condone or excuse the actions of others wrong. Instead, it involves letting go of the bad feelings from the wrongdoing. It also involves moving toward well-being. He included that asking friends and family for support can be crucial to forgiveness.

His coworkers assumed he had no life story because of his early age. They believed that adversity had not shaped him into a young man. And so, they undertook, he had no strategies for overcoming what he had not experienced. Hardships, problematic situations, and misfortunes are all examples of trouble. Anyone can encounter problems, regardless of background, age, or life path.

Again, age has no address for trials and tribulations. When a believer struggles to rise above adversity, anger holds them in. And it is because of unforgiveness. The person who got the outburst did not cause stress or pain. It was inevitable. It is essential to be aware of anger's effects, as it can lead to stress, anxiety, and irritability. The overwhelming frustration can induce a sense of powerlessness.

However, the perception of forgiveness can vary by culture, religion, and views. One way to gauge the trustworthiness of information is to be aware of its source. For example, it is never too late to change course. If you catch yourself in the middle of overthinking, do an about-face.

1. Apologize to the victim of your eruption.
2. Close your eyes and take a deep breath, allowing your mind to clear.
3. If it is within your power, we encourage you to find a quiet place to be alone for a few minutes.

But only after Jocephus gave his life to Jesus. Then, he found a sure way to rise above hardship and cope with life's difficulties. He learned to embrace life's storms. He overcame adversity with the guidance of the Author and Perfecter of his faith. The writer found that beating adversity and facing unforeseen obstacles is life's essence. It is the message of The Hope of Glory (Colossians 1:27).

When supporters of Christ address problems, it means confronting them with determination. Without a doubt, this takes resilience. This approach does not shy away from hardships. It would help if you embraced them. Seek fixes and take bold actions to conquer them.

So, how one responds to adversity gauges one's character. For example, concrete lays a building's foundation. Christian life experiences lay the foundation for your skills, outlook, and abilities. The ability to be brave and work hard is something you gain over time, not something with which you are born. The Saints earned their skills through righteousness by overcoming adversity.

Christians must triumph over hardship. They must beat the obstacles that hinder them. The Glorified adapting to challenging situations and maintaining performance, also known as flexibility, is essential. It demands honest self-evaluation, acknowledging and improving your limitations. As they rise above adversity, it is about seeking support and learning from others. The Bible says that past challenges can improve a person. They can help them bounce back from tough times and do well.

We can rejoice when we face problems and trials. They help us build endurance. Endurance builds character. Character strengthens our hope of salvation. (Romans 5:3-4).

When life gets tough, rising above means pressing through and overcoming pitfalls. It is about not quitting when faced with trials and beating them in the Name of Jesus. The Apostle Paul says, "He presses toward the goal to win the prize. GOD called him to heaven in Christ" (Philippians 3:14). The key is faith in The LORD to press through the tough times. Every damaging, struggling experience allows Christians to learn and become stronger.

"Blessed is the one who endures trials, for they will receive the crown of life promised by GOD to those who love him." James 1:12.

Supporters of Jesus Christ can rise above enemies. They do this by finding purpose in every experience. It allows us to uncover valuable lessons hidden deep within. Christians find meaning in their experiences. They can better cope with stress and adversity. They find comfort in the sounds of hymns and prayers. Finding meaning gives strength to overcome life's challenges. The Saints must recognize the significance of their lives beyond themselves. Jesus Christ provides a framework for understanding challenges and setbacks.

As Christians, accepting the greater meaning of one's life is crucial. Turning to Jesus' teachings for comfort in challenging times is critical. Righteous beliefs encourage the pursuit of a higher purpose through this perspective. It also teaches finding strength in faith, not problems.

In Christian theology, the teachings of Jesus Christ often focus on principles. These include love, compassion, forgiveness, and resilience in challenges. The instructions give comfort and guidance to many Christians. They help Christians navigate life's trials. Many religions and philosophies stress a purpose beyond oneself. They prompt people to think about the greater good and others' welfare.

Finally, let's shift our view. Let's see challenges as chances for growth and learning, not obstacles. Rather than thinking, "I cannot do this," let's change our mindset. We see that "as I face challenges, I can conquer them with Christ's help." Instead of fixating on past errors, let's focus on the gained knowledge. Then, we can apply it to wiser choices ahead. Instead of saying, "This is too difficult," let's welcome the challenge. Let's trust that our efforts will bring success and personal growth.

When confronted with setbacks, let's view them as temporary obstacles, not lasting defeats. Every small step progresses in the right direction. Let's shift our mindset from doubt to righteous affirmation. Remember, progress matters more than perfection. Therefore, adopting a righteous and cheerful outlook can give us confidence. It can also offer us with the resilience in our goals.

Again, challenges become steppingstones, and setbacks become opportunities to refine our strategies. So, embracing this view empowers us to oversee adversity with GOD's grace and determination. It fosters a mindset that leads to success and boosts our well-being.

CHAPTER 13

Accomplishment should not be the ultimate destination but a steppingstone to greatness.

The Challenge

It is crucial to acknowledge that Christians face different difficulties. These differ based on their situations, where they live, and their culture. Yet, some familiar challenges that Christians may experience include:

Some places persecute Christians for their faith through ethnic cleansing. It can range from discrimination and social exclusion to physical violence and imprisonment.

Christians could face obstacles in society. Their beliefs and values differ from the prevailing norms. It can create conflict and hardships in one's daily routine.

Skepticism and marginalization of religious beliefs create challenges. They affect Christians in more secular societies. It can manifest in educational institutions or the workplace. Skepticism is an attitude of doubt or questioning toward knowledge, beliefs, or claims. It involves inspecting information, ideas, or arguments. It comprises a reluctance to accept Christianity at face value without enough evidence.

Christians face ethical and moral dilemmas. They grapple with reconciling their beliefs with modern values. Its application in technology, bioethics, and social justice magnifies its significance in two ways:

a. INTERFAITH RELATIONS: Fostering understanding and tolerance between different religious communities is hard. It is like breaking through steel barriers. Christians may face difficulties. They must promote peace and dialogue in areas with many religions.

b. INTERNAL DENOMINATIONAL DIFFERENCES: There are many denominations with varying theological perspectives within Christianity. Navigating these differences and keeping unity can be challenging for Christians. It is valid for Christians as individuals and as a group.

Christians may wrestle with secular values and popular culture. These clash with their religious beliefs. This clash is because of globalization and secular influences in our interconnected world.

But the title shows that Christians will face many temptations. They must follow GOD's teachings. They will face more than what he listed. Paul writes in First Corinthians 10:13, "No temptation has overtaken us. It is what is common to humanity. And GOD is faithful; He will not allow temptations beyond what we can bear. But when temptation comes, The LORD will also give a way out so His people can endure it." In the above verse, Paul suggests that the Infinite Spirit strengthens believers. It also gives them the means to overcome challenges.

He also implies that Jehovah provides a way out. So, this is for when believers face temptation or challenges. The Apostle's message encourages Christians to rely on GOD's strength. They should trust in His faithfulness during tough times. It also emphasizes that GOD understands the human experience. He is helping believers overcome trials. Different Christian groups and people may interpret this verse in several ways. But they agree it conveys hope, assurance, and trust in GOD's support. It is for all believers in challenging times.

Overcoming problems for anybody is a normal part of life. But the Author and Perfecter of Our Faith (Hebrews 12: 2) gives the Saints many strategies. They help to navigate difficulties so His people can overcome them. Here are general tips that may help:

1. "The joy of The LORD is our strength." (Nehemiah 8:10). A pleasant mindset cultivates a righteous outlook when dealing with difficult predicaments. Praying about problems often will help us hear more from GOD. It will also help us align His actions with ours. For instance, we focus on what we can control. We look for growth in every challenge. A sanctified mindset about troubles will enhance our resilience.

2. Study First Peter verses 5:6, 7. It tells us to humble ourselves under GOD's mighty hand so he may lift us in time. He wants us to cast all our anxiety on Him because He cares for us. GOD shows us to break challenges into smaller tasks. It tackles one problem at a time. Therefore, this makes the whole challenge less scary and more doable. So, do not be afraid to give The LORD your problems. In Titus 2:13, we share with Our Great GOD and Savior. This sharing provides us with varied views and valuable insights.

3. Learn from stumbling blocks and view them as chances to learn and grow. Ask the Blessed and Only Ruler (1 Timothy 6:15) what went wrong. Then, use that knowledge to adjust your approach to move forward. Setbacks are part of life. Everyone faced delays, interruptions, postponements, and disappointment. Jesus's words are: "Be ready for trials and tribulations" in John 16:33: "I have told you these things so that in me you may have peace." "You will have trouble. But take heart! I have overcome the world."

Although stumbling blocks are a normal part of life, every believer has a choice to allow them to define us. Or are we faithful enough to choose to see the setback as a moment for GOD to aid us in converting them into a revival? We can turn to GOD for support in triumphing over any setback. Listen, we characterized battle tension and conflicts. We struggle to control our thoughts, schedules, families, and places of worship. Even our community work is a site of ongoing conflicts in our society.

Feeling let down, turned away, or unsure of where to go or what to do can lead to discouragement. Yet, by learning to embrace it and have trust in The Author of Life (Acts 3: 15), our faith can grow deeper. Once we surpass the obstacle, we can spread the joy of victory to so many others! 2 Corinthians 10:4 suggests that the weapons we use in our battles differ from those used in the world. On the inverse, they have Divine power to demolish strongholds."

We can learn to turn challenging situations into triumphs. We do this by studying the problem's strategy through prayer. Joshua was a formidable warrior. He won many battles. He excelled at defeating supernatural forces.

An example is his conquest of Jericho in Joshua 6:27. It says: "So GOD was with Joshua, and his fame spread." The victory at Jericho shows the vast favor that GOD has given to Joshua and Israel. They were unstoppable!

4. Embrace adaptability by remaining flexible and open to adjusting your strategies. Challenges cause a shift in approach. Being adaptable can increase one's chance of success. It involves being flexible, open-minded, and able to learn. You must develop in response to new challenges or situations. The writer sees adaptability as valuable. It is critical in his life, including personal growth, work, and problem-solving. It lets him manage uncertainties and take advantage of opportunities.

5. Take care of yourself physically and mentally. You must prioritize enough rest, exercise, and relaxation. Leisure time is suitable for a healthy life. A sound foundation contributes to better problem-solving. Remember, self-care is a personal journey. It is vital to tailor it to your needs and preferences. By taking care of yourself, you can improve your life. It will also give you a base for solving problems and being tough when facing difficulties.

Note the more we fixate on challenges, the harder they are to oversee. And the more we desire them. Our passion for these challenges only grows more formidable. The law of attraction applies to this view. Our energy and attention can affect our experiences. When faced with challenges, being preoccupied presents a learning opportunity. It will make them seem scarier than they are. Then we play the WISH GAME LOOP in our heads. For instance,

1. I wish I had not said that dumb thing to my boss.
2. I wish I had volunteered for that project, now winning awards.
3. I wish I had spoken up to myself.
4. I wish I had not messed up with them; they could have been clients.
5. I wish I had not told my husband/wife that stupid thing.

The Bible emphasizes: "Submit to GOD and resist" temptation (James 4: 7) by doing righteous meditation. It can stimulate your inner Spirit. The Holy Writ shows that virtuous meditation can help the Saint. It can help them contemplate Holiness, avoid seduction, and find peace. Scripture study endows us with grit, might, and joy.

But "self-blame" is self-abuse. It means people hold themselves accountable. Note this is for a mistake, failure, or problem. It is counterproductive. It distracts us from addressing the issues and finding solutions. The blame game is typical in many contexts. It often leads to angry and unproductive chatter.

Or they were replaying spiritual truths in our heads. However, connecting with the Divine will lead to profound joy. The Scriptures inspire. They offer hope and guidance. They lead to lasting happiness beyond temporary joys. Yet, Word study brings joy regardless of dire external circumstances. Also, as we reflect on Scripture, it is transformative. It is enriching and brings forth many virtues. It imbues individuals with grit, might, and joy. For example,

1. "And the peace of GOD, which transcends all understanding, will guard your hearts and minds in Christ Jesus."

   Philippians 4:7

2. "Finally, brothers, think about whatever is honorable and pure. Also, think about whatever is lovely and commendable. If there is any excellence or praiseworthy, think about these things."

   Philippians 4:8

3. "If you have embraced Christ, look for the things above, where Christ sits at the right hand of GOD."

   Colossians 3:1

4. "Set your minds on things above, not on things on earth."

   Colossians 3:2

5. Be joyful, my brothers, when facing many trials. You know that assessing your faith makes you steadfast. And let commitment have its full effect, that you may be perfect and complete, lacking in nothing."

   James 1:2-4

Listen, Spiritual meditation means connecting with GOD. He is beyond humanity's challenges. It is the ultimate cure for obstacles. The Saints should remember that The LORD is more significant than any problem. So, we can overcome any challenge by seeking His help and having faith in His power. Each obstacle and difficulty is a chance to seek GOD's help. We can use our creative talent, intelligence, and Holy intensity.

To connect with the Resurrection of Life, you must cultivate Holy mindfulness. Do this even if you feel inconsistent. Contemplating within oneself involves self-examination and scrutinizing one's thoughts, actions, and beliefs. It is about knowing your strengths and weaknesses. It is about seeing inconsistencies and seeking personal growth. This growth is through the Mediator of the New Covenant (Hebrews 9:15). This process can lead to a deeper understanding of oneself. It can also lead to a connection to The LORD's purpose for a more meaningful life.

The Glorified must admit their mistakes to succeed in our meditation/prayer. They must strive to be honest. However, different religions have unique ways of practicing prayer meditation. But Christians limit their prayerful reflection to their faith. They have faith in the Deity of Jesus Christ. Prayer is the means of talking to GOD. Christians focus their prayer on Jesus. He is the Atoning Sacrifice for Our sins and challenges (1 John 2:2). His supporters seek His guidance and forgiveness. They thank Him for His sacrifice to atone for humanity's sins.

Christ's meditation helps us understand life's challenges. It also makes us more determined to aid others. Kindness, power, and humility mark spiritual wisdom. Yet, the journey to spiritual awareness through meditation takes time. Spiritual realization needs discipline and practice, but adding patience has significant benefits. Among its advantages is reducing stress and anxiety. The writer believes patience has improved his self-esteem, social skills, and cognitive health.

Still, the world's details call on us. They require us to do challenging mental and physical tasks. Thus, an individual's problems may seem impossible. But if they press through them in Jesus' name. Troubles can strengthen one's faith (Philippians 3:14). And carry Saints beyond their limits. It teaches them essential life lessons about endurance. Problems build our resilience and teach us how to cope with tricky situations. Believers can reach their full potential through difficulties and adversity.

Still, it is understandable to avoid confronting life's tough challenges. However, evading problems does not lead to solutions; it only delays the inevitable. Nonetheless, voiding or running from problems may give temporary relief. But it rarely leads to lasting fixes. It can make things more difficult. Please understand facing challenges does not mean confronting them without a plan. It involves thoughtful and prayerful consideration. It needs strategic problem-solving. Seek support when needed and learn from the experience.

Thus, when we see challenges as opportunities for growth, it helps. Problem-solving can lead to long-term success and fulfillment. An enthusiastic challenge will energize and improve your mindset. Troubleshooting issues will also help us grow as leaders, learners, and people. Challenges are obstacles to overcome and opportunities for growth, learning, and personal development. Embracing challenges with a positive mindset can lead to significant changes. They can help you become a better Christian.

Confronting challenges is critical for growth. It is crucial to face them, even when uncomfortable. Doing so builds resilience. It allows individuals to develop coping skills, problem-solving abilities, and emotional strength. Still, ignoring problems could lead to individual decay and becoming more complicated. However, facing challenges head-on can provide a sense of accomplishment and empowerment. It helps people learn from experience. They understand themselves and their world better.

Still, it is natural to want to avoid pain. But facing life's challenges in Christ can lead to more meaningful outcomes. They will also be more fulfilling. So, keep a positive mindset. Focus on solutions, not problems. This approach is better. Again, seek support from friends, family, or pros. It can make facing challenges easier.

Harsh conditions will be our comrade often. They will be with us a lot. No matter how hard we try, it is impossible to escape them. The only thing left to ponder is our reaction, so how will we react to them? Our challenges and obstacles could be growth opportunities. Yet, Jesus is the only way for Christians to keep going. He helps them turn tough times into progress.

By accepting challenges, one can cultivate patience, modesty, and fortitude. The Bible says GOD will establish us. He will also strengthen and settle us after a brief period of suffering. Patience, perseverance, and faith are all virtues learned through trials. Faith is a firm belief in Jehovah or the Scriptures. It is based on spiritual intuition, not on proof. Divine forbearance allows the Holy Spirit to show us how to resist temptation.

Everyone faces the allure of sin, no matter their experience with Christ. It is a constant obstacle to overcome. Despite this, we can try to boost our righteous flexibility. We can also increase our capacity to combat wrongdoing. The writer uses five Biblical methods to help him overcome challenging temptations.

1. He seeks prayer
2. Read the Bible
3. Connect with other Christian
4. Acknowledge sin
5. He understands that his sinful nature can lure him to sin

As per James 1:14, a believer who tempts others is an excuse for supporters to oppose GOD's Law. But they stray from the truth, virtue, and GOD's standard of righteousness. Listen, the evil framework desires are like a powerful magnet. They pull the Saints onto a path of ruin.

Then, the urge to defy or devalue the Christian faith leads to destruction. We have an insatiable thirst for wickedness. When someone offers us Gospel hope, we may feel tempted by food, drink, sex, money, drugs, or fun. In the Apostle's Epistle, James defines temptation as a distraction. It leads to sin by drawing us from prohibited things. So, the first step to overcoming temptation is to know it seduces our cravings.

Those who walk in the flesh produce the fruits of the flesh. These include sexual immorality, idolatry, jealousy, and more" (Galatians 5:20-21).

But those who walk in the Spirit "will not gratify the desires of the flesh" (Galatians 5:16).

GOD's grace alone saves us from the desires of the flesh through Jesus Christ, with no credit to ourselves. Understanding sanctification increases responsibility and the desire to glorify Him. It explains the grief we feel. We feel it when we realize we have failed to satisfy the Divine.

CHAPTER 14

It is beneficial not to let your spirit dwell on its challenges. Instead, give everything to GOD and let Him work His Glory.

Spiritual Distractions

If you are struggling to focus, you are not alone. Mindless diversions also hurt our focus. However, Colossians 3:2 emphasizes, "Set our mind on things above, not things of the earth."

We know the things as spiritual distractions. They divert our thoughts from the Holy Spirit. Today, the world is complete with countless distractions. They compete for the Christian's attention. This competition desensitizes us to many external stimuli. It disconnects us from our spiritual core. The Author of Life (Acts 3:15) teaches His disciples, "That whoever abides in him can bear much fruit." Study John Chapters Fourteen through Sixteen.

But Jesus says another reliable truth we can trust. He adverts: "Apart from me, you can do nothing." Those who do not follow Jesus cannot join in His life or help His mission. Like fruitless trees, He collects and incinerates them (John 15:6).

"Abide in me" is the phrase Jesus uses to describe a life focused on him. Apart from that focus on Christ, believers have vulnerability. For instance, we disengage from what is happening. So, a bitter heart is coming. It will interfere with our Holy focus.

We dedicate energy to something. It influences its growth. The quality of attention and energy matters as much as the quantity. Focusing, minding, and purpose in your efforts can enhance your success. Balancing attention and energy is critical. One must pay attention to several aspects of life. Christian well-being and holistic growth depend on this crucial aspect.

So, be mindful. Worldly connectivity can distract us and make us lose our connection with Jehovah. Too, others can get hurt because of our disobedience. Take Jonah as an example. Jonah 1:3 shows this. His decision to run from GOD caused his life to go downhill. We will face the same consequences when we turn from Christ, The Hope of Glory and King Eternal, as in 1 Timothy 1:17.

GOD's omnipresence means that no matter how fast you try to run, you can never escape Him. Trying to do it would be a waste of time and effort. Again, no matter how hard one tries, you cannot run away from the Almighty. He is always pursuing you with affection.

The Book of Jonah shows us how disobedience will cost us money and hurt us physically. It can also harm those around us. Specifically, the ship and the sailors were in a dangerous place. It was all because of Jonah being on board the vessel. Jonah confesses his presence on board is causing the storm. So, they follow his request, and the crew throws him overboard, resulting in the storm subsiding.

Even though the sailors could be present on the ship, Jonah had no valid excuse for his presence. The story highlights the consequences of his disobedience and how he ended up in the belly of a great fish. The situation was not ideal. But it would have been okay for him to travel to Tarshish under different conditions.

Today, some Christians choose to distance themselves from GOD. By disobeying, they achieve this. In their eyes, they can coexist with transgressions considered "minor" or "acceptable." They think these do not require salvation or are not as bad as the "major" ones, such as murder and adultery.

But we get distracted when we look away from Jesus, the Faithful and True Witness in Revelation 3:14-15. We shift our focus to something else. The problem is this. People believe Americans are joining the Church less, as the trend shows. They do fewer Christ-centered things. These include belonging to a denomination. They also include attending worship services and asking The LORD for forgiveness.

So, Immanuel's supporters underestimate sin. Because of this, they minimize the importance of repentance. In Christian theology, sin is primary. Repentance is crucial to the Christian faith. Repentance involves three things. You must acknowledge and turn away from sin. You must seek forgiveness and strive for a better life.

Yet, secularism is a challenge for the Saints. It leads them to neglect their Christian duties. Rebellious thinking will bankrupt the Saints' righteousness. It will also strain their relationship with The Father. The result could distract them. It would keep them from resolving issues that need Holy solutions. For instance, we neglect the Seven Gifts of the Holy Spirit. They are Wisdom, understanding, Counsel, Fortitude, Knowledge, Piety, and fear of The LORD.

We will share more about these gifts below, but for now:

Neglecting our spiritual gifts can make us empty and detached. We become detached from our true identities in Christ. He atoned for our sins (1 John 2: 2). This neglect hinders our personal and spiritual progress. Then, we look for a reason for distractions from our Christian responsibility. Spiritual gifts are unique abilities. Skilled believers have them. They use them to grow and help others succeed.

Spiritual psychology studies the bond between the human mind and the spirit world. They are concurrent. For secular people, spiritual psychologists are vital. They help incorporate the mind, body, and spirit into daily life. This comprehensive approach helps overcome difficulties. Sometimes, they teach their clients to let go of—anything that disturbs their peace.

Yet, as Christians, we learn to overcome challenges. We do this through the great power given by the Holy Spirit. For instance, the above gifts connect Christians to parts of our lives. They connect to the lives of others, the Local Church, and the whole Body of Christ.

Every Christian must focus on finding their GOD-given mind and understanding it. Thus, without Divine gifts, we lose inner fulfillment. We miss chances to help others and to stay focused.

The Sacred gifts strengthen, motivate, and give counsel to the Church. GOD gives His supporters talents to help the Body of Christ. (1 Corinthians 12:7) refers to the "common good". Sacred gifts also help to keep the Saints focused.

They clarify Christ is their beliefs' primary focus, emphasizing his importance. They believe they can reach the highest level. Because of this, they surround themselves with like-minded Saints. The Saints believe in their abilities. They stay focused on their goals. They avoid distractions or deviations from their right path.

Also, spiritual gifts are critical of Christianity for personal growth and well-being. They also help with a deeper connection with Jesus, the "Alpha and Omega" (Revelation 1:8; 22:13). Without these abilities, the Saints will feel empty. They will lack purpose. They will feel disconnected from a power that is greater than secularism. Living a Christian life can be challenging because of this.

Do not misunderstand: If the Holy Spirit dwells in you, He endows you with all His gifts. But the act of using them is a separate issue altogether. In Christian teachings, the Divine Spirit is the third person of the Holy Trinity. The Spirit is with GOD, The Father, and the Son (Jesus Christ). He empowers and guides believers, providing them with unique abilities.

Below, the writer summarizes the importance of giving talent for free. These are akin to the gift of the Spirit. The writer does this by exposing their supporting ideas and human intelligence. Wherever the Holy Spirit's powers are present, people will feel sin. They will repent. We call this, for example:

1. The Holy Spirit designed the gift of Christian conviction. It aims to bring confession, repentance, and renewal of humanity's relationship with GOD. The Holy Spirit's role is to show sin. He guides sinners to the grace of Christ in the Gospel.

, we focus on the bigger picture, which is righteousness. This focus helps us avoid getting caught up in unimportant details. Such details do not contribute to our aim of Christianity. In Christianity, focusing on the bigger picture means prioritizing love. It also means compassion, forgiveness, and obeying Jesus' teachings.

Christian convictions suggest looking beyond minor disagreements or disruptions. These may arise. Instead, focus on the central tenets of the faith. And repent the wrongs and distractions that cause us to deviate from our faith.

Distraction is an action that hinders us from what we want. The difference seems obvious, but the distraction is sneaky. It is hard to tell if we are moving towards or away from what we must do today.

So, keeping one's eyes on the goal follows Christianity. Christianity emphasizes following GOD's will. These broader principles are about righteousness. They can help people find purpose and guidance. It provides them with a compass to navigate the intricate web of life's challenges.

When Bettye and I started our relationship sixty years ago, we had a mutual understanding. We did this by acknowledging our roles in failed relationships. We repented our past and vowed not to bring them into our future. It suggests self-awareness and a commitment to learning from past mistakes. These can help with future distractions. They also help with the success and length of the relationship.

For a strong partnership, it is essential to keep nurturing open communication. Trust, respect, and forgiveness have been vital over the years. Someone in your life keeps bringing up their failed relationship. They lack a sense of security when you are around.

Bettye and I took a thoughtful and mature approach to building our relationship. We did it by acknowledging past mistakes and focusing on Christ-centered principles. It keeps us focused on the broader principles of right. It helps us avoid getting stuck with tiny details of life. Then we included:

a. Spending critical time with each other at Church.
b. After that, the discussion shifted its focus to future events instead of dwelling on the past.
c. We both got to know each other's friends. Besides, this is a waving red flag when someone refuses to introduce you to their close friends. It implies they feel embarrassed to inform your acquaintances about your existence.

Following the above points, we have shared our thoughts and Christian beliefs. We did this over half a century of marriage.

But how does considering the broader view of salvation help us love others more? It helps us stay focused. There are four approaches to this:

- Studying Christian beliefs can help us understand others. We can learn about their challenges, experiences, and feelings. This gift of Sacred wisdom promotes empathy. It lets us focus on "The things that are true, honest, right, clean, and pure. Things are lovely and good to talk about." When they are honorable, we can pivot to and recognize the feelings and hardships others face.
- Moral empathy expands our view. We see humankind within a broader framework of what is right. Cognitive compassion increases the likelihood of helping others and showing

kindness. Sacred judgment empowers us to nurture kindness. It does this by seeing the shared human experience. And by seeking happiness.

- Scripture intelligence assists us in acknowledging diversity. A clear view lets us see differences. It accepts individual variations. The Holy Writ will help us see this. It will show that everyone has unique backgrounds, values, and views. It will foster a more inclusive and tolerant mindset. Valuing differences and promoting inclusivity will help us. They will help us focus on a more open understanding. It will help us understand the unsaved.

- Holy prudence encourages forgiveness. It helps us understand why people behave the way they do. Empathizing with their intentions makes forgiving them easier. Recognizing that everyone makes mistakes or struggles helps. It allows us to let go of resentment and promote forgiveness. Forgiveness is a gift. It keeps us focused on building better relationships. It also helps us improve mental health. And it reduces anxiety, stress, and hostility.

- The gift of foresight is the quality of being wise and leads us to contemplate GOD's profound mysteries. It shows us the core principles of our Evangelical faith. It reminds us why we serve the great GOD. Through observation, we learn about our beliefs that move us beyond faith. Christian foreknowledge helps our beliefs and ignores the voice of distrust.

Holy perceptiveness reminds us never to forget. It shows us what parts of faithfulness are essential to us. It also reminds us of the challenges we may face in moving past the basic teachings of Christ (Hebrews 6: 1-3). Thus, acknowledgment or awareness makes us see our core values. They are values of sanctification. They involve the pursuit of Holiness when life's challenges are imminent.

All the above energy appears again in Jesus. It comes through His suffering in the Garden of Gethsemane and on the cross. He mastered every challenge we faced. It keeps our focus on Him. He faced them through His death, burial, and resurrection.

Because of His humanity, The LORD understands human emotions and struggles. His grace will empower us to conquer them and keep us focused on His Divinity. Yet, we must grasp His idea. We do this by turning to Jesus Christ. It will fortify our understanding and offer stability during challenging times.

Righteous percipience is a framework of six theological concepts. The writer aims to show below how each view can affect the Saints' lives. They help the Saints remain steadfast when they have the gift of Holy insight. These six Christian theological elements are:

I. Apologetics is the Sacred discipline of defending Christian doctrines. It relies on systematic arguments and discourse. The early Christian apologists taught us how to protect our faith. They also taught us to promote our beliefs to others. It is a rational way to address people's objections to Christianity. It does this through systematic, argumentative discourse and keeps us interested.

Also, the writer can say this. GOD used Christian apologetics to sharpen and deepen his faith.

When he felt unprepared or lacked confidence, he looked to Jesus.

When unprepared, he behaved in a Holy manner.

The author taught Seminary classes to parishioners on how to defend the faith. Nonetheless, he is confident in evangelism and faith perseverance. But he sometimes lacks the discipline of apologetics. It makes him unhappy but motivates him to make changes and develop himself to improve.

II. DISCERNMENT is the model to clarify and justify one's convictions. Explaining and justifying convictions shows attentive comprehension. This process requires comprehension, coherent expression, and evidential support for our stance. Righteous perceptiveness is crucial for believers in critical thinking and effective communication.

For example, the Apostle Peter delves into the details in his writings. He explains the Christian faith. In your hearts, honor Christ, The LORD, as Holy. Always be ready to defend it to anyone who asks for a reason for your hope. But do it with gentleness and respect." (1 Peter 3:15). This is impossible to do. It needs the Holy Spirit's extraordinary powers.

III. Not to repeat. BIBLICAL INTERPRETATION explains the meaning of Christian dogmas. This facet focuses on comprehending the significance and implications of righteous concepts. Holy elucidation goes beyond what someone has recalled. It involves using understanding to solve problems or address the "Ontology" of Scripture. You need not let questions about GOD or His universe distract you.

IV. The gift of INSIGHT gives us a broader perspective on consecration. It allows us the ability to consider and adopt various viewpoints. This facet encourages people to see things from different angles. It also enables them to understand diverse views on a topic.

Open-mindedness is the capacity to assess and embrace different outlooks. They resist New Testament ideas and hold old wives› traditions. They have lost their connection with the Holy Spirit.

A Saint should be open-minded. They will listen to different viewpoints and consider other opinions. They will change their views based on unknown facts or insights. Hallowed Sagaciousness is valuable for consecrated observation. It fosters excellent communication, teamwork, and personal growth. It lets people have constructive talks and widen their view of human issues.

Appreciation is also a path to empathy. It is about valuing others' feelings, thoughts, and views. When used, it can dispel lots of argumentative challenges. This component emphasizes the human and emotional aspects of gratitude. It is about witnessing Christ to sinners.

Encouragement is vital. It means seeing, understanding others, and welcoming their feelings, thoughts, and objectivity.

It goes beyond courtesy and mere acknowledgment. Incentive involves telling that person you appreciate them. You thank them for letting you share Jesus' salvation. Valuing this way is also crucial for forming close and deep connections with others. It fosters compassion and builds good relationships. The gift of appreciation is critical to creating a more compassionate world.

In Christianity, whether personal or professional, empathy leads to excellent outcomes. Christian friendship helps the well-being of people and society. It is a critical quality. Righteous, tender-heartedness can cause positive social change and kinder relationships.

VI. Linking self-knowledge and understanding. Our motives drive our pursuit of clarity and confidence. We seek to ensure that our self-concept reflects our genuine goodness.

So, for Christians, self-knowledge means being aware of who we are in Jesus Christ. It also means considering our cognitive processes, biases, and limits. It involves the act of introspection and acknowledging areas that require enhancement.

One example is the need to understand your strengths and weaknesses. Follow a path that uses your strengths. Face challenges to it. Doing this can unlock spiritual growth.

So, knowing ourselves and admitting our sins can bring us closer to Jesus Christ and the Holy Spirit. It can also give us a greater sense of personal focus and serenity about our place in the world. Consecrated self-awareness lets us get closer to GOD. It allows us to become our best selves, as GOD intended.

These six aspects are a complete way to assess and improve a deep understanding of the life of Christ. They urge Christian educators to move beyond memorization. They should focus on fostering actual knowledge of the Gospel.

For example, in Chapter 6, verses 1-3, the Hebrew author tells believers to go beyond the basics. They should move past teachings about repentance, faith, baptism, etc.

The Gospel writer prioritizes spiritual growth and maturity. He emphasizes that spiritual growth is a slow journey. You cannot achieve it overnight, nor is it an end. To mature spiritually, you must exert effort and practice discipline. You must also make sacrifices and persevere in pursuing the goal. The Saints cannot take shortcuts.

The Seven Gifts of the Holy Spirit help fight off the problem. False Gospels circulate alongside Christianity. These are Gnosticism and Hermeticism. They are ancient belief systems that explore the mysteries of the universe. These factors complicated the expansion of Christianity.

That said. Every Christian should know the Seven Gifts of the Holy Spirit that makes them Holy. They make recipients docile to the Spirit of Jesus. It contributes to their development of Holiness and readiness for heaven. We can trace them back to the Book of Isaiah, which patristic authors have analyzed. Again, among them are:

a. Wisdom
b. Understanding
c. Counsel
d. Fortitude
e. Knowledge
f. Piety
g. Fear of THE LORD

1. The gift of DIVINE WISDOM enables one to make wise choices. Knowledge, experience, and understanding do this. It requires expertise to solve real-world problems. Common sense involves considering the long-term impact and ethical aspects of actions. Wisdom surpasses intelligence and learning. It includes empathy, knowledge of human nature, and balanced decision-making. The gift of discernment/wisdom is a link to maturity. It is also a link to insight and the ability to understand complex situations.

   Divine wisdom surpasses mere intelligence and education. It includes a deep understanding of empathy, human nature, and ethics. It implies wise choices based on knowledge, experience, and a broader perspective. Righteous enlightenment keeps GOD's people focused. It brings structure to their goals and objectives.

   Heavenly foresight is a gift given by the Almighty. It involves a connection to a higher source of knowledge. This source guides people in navigating life's challenges. It does so with a sense of purpose and moral clarity. Maturity, insight, and the skill to manage complex situations link wisdom. An individual does it with a balanced and discerning approach.

   Divine wisdom shows that true wisdom is not intelligent. It needs a complete understanding. This understanding must consider the ethical and emotional parts of decision-making.

2. The LORD gives the gift of Christian understanding to supporters of Jesus Christ. It gives them the ability to grasp the meaning of sanctification. They can understand its significance and nature.

   Thoughtful perception allows us to analyze data, establish connections, and understand the topic. So, Divine comprehension surpasses awareness and requires integrating knowledge, context, and experience to form a meaningful interpretation. Analysis, synthesis, and critical thinking are cognitive processes that help us focus and can lead to achievement. Understanding revolves around the ability of supporters of Jesus Christ to comprehend and appreciate the meaning, significance, or nature of various aspects of sanctification.

Stressing righteousness requires more than awareness. It needs analyzing data, making connections, and a deep understanding. Comprehension goes beyond gaining knowledge. It adds context and firsthand experiences to form a meaning.

In the Christian view, understanding is a gift from The LORD. It involves thoughtful engagement with the subject. Common sense goes beyond surface-level awareness to form a deep and meaningful interpretation. The processes imply a more engaged approach to learning and interpreting information.

3. COUNSEL is a spiritual concept within Christianity. It is like a beacon of proper judgment, a priceless treasure. The Holy Spirit nudges us to make good choices. It uses this gift to guide us and keep us from distractions. Christians can defend the truths of the faith without fear, relying on the gift of counsel. Jesus, the Advocate, known as the 'Counselor,' will offer unwavering guidance.

Jehovah, the Holy Spirit, grants the gift of counsel for righteous decision-making. The Divine admonition is a source of proper judgment and guidance. It is akin to a beacon that illuminates the path of goodness. It keeps our minds on Holiness. The gift lets Christians defend their faith. It also allows them to make choices that align with their beliefs.

The name 'Counselor' or 'Advocate' for the Holy Spirit comes from the Bible. It comes from the teachings of Jesus in the New Testament. In the Gospel of John, Jesus speaks about the coming of the Holy Spirit as a helper and guide. Believers can rely on the Spirit to help them focus on one task at a time and avoid distractions.

4. The gift of Fortitude captures the Spirit of bravery, fearlessness, and determination. With this talent, individuals defend GOD and proclaim His truths. Those with grit will face evil. Righteous courage will support sound doctrine when needed. Believers fix their minds on righteousness. They do this like a laser locked onto its target.

    The suggestion is that gifted individuals commit to righteousness. They are unwavering in pursuing it. Afresh, the image is of a laser beam locked onto its target. It implies a focused and unyielding dedication to their faith's principles. This idea matches many religions. They stress courage and steadfastness in challenges. Christian determination is accurate when facing what they see as evil or defending truths.

    The gift of Fortitude inspires believers to act with resilience and moral conviction. Their faith and a sense of righteousness guide them.

5. The Gift of Knowledge lets believers grasp the deep meaning and intention of GOD. It gives them the strength to embrace and live out this purpose. Unlike wisdom, it demands more than a desire. Grace's cognition needs an active commitment to living through GOD's teachings. It sets itself apart from understanding by being more than a skill. It is an inherent understanding that comes from within.

    The spiritual concept of the Gift of Knowledge is religious. It stresses the gift's importance. It helps believers understand GOD's purpose in their lives. Embracing this goes beyond a wish. It demands a firm commitment to live by GOD's teachings. The Gift of Knowledge differs from wisdom and experience. It is broader and goes beyond mere skill.

    Spiritual gifts such as knowledge, wisdom, and understanding are blessings in Christianity. These gifts strengthen believers' bond with the Divine. They guide them to live meaningful lives based on their faith.

6. Piety is another of the Holy Spirit's gifts. It symbolizes the peak of Christian devotion and unwavering loyalty. It means getting rid of distractions. Today, Christianity is a set of external practices. But piety goes beyond rituals. It represents a profound devotion to worship and serve GOD.

   It exemplifies unwavering loyalty to the Almighty, binding supporters through vows and obligations. But more than that, it takes believers beyond duty. It inspires a deep desire to worship The LORD and serve Him out of love. Like the way, we desire to honor our parents and fulfill their wishes.

   Again, piety goes beyond rituals. Holiness shows a deep devotion to worship and serve GOD. It emphasizes unwavering loyalty to GOD. Righteousness binds believers through vows and obligations.

   This view agrees with the traditional Christian understanding of Christian purity. Piety involves a deep and sincere commitment to spiritual life. People mark this life with prayer, reverence, and service. It highlights the personal and emotional aspects of one's relationship with the Divine. It emphasizes a connection beyond mere duty.

7. When one has a healthy fear of The LORD, it allows for a proper perspective on righteousness. Supporters of Jesus with this gift understand the greatness and awesomeness of Jesus. He is The Hope of Glory, the Eternal King (1 Timothy 1:17). They want to serve Him because of His awe-inspiring Divine Nature. The gift of fear of The LORD fills people with awe and reverence. It helps them find their true selves and understand their Divine purpose.

Let us delve deeper into THE fear of The LORD's meaning. Most Western Christian pastors see fear as an unpleasant emotion. It comes from the belief that someone or something is dangerous. So, at an agnostic conference, you are more likely to hear about the Fear of GOD than at most Local Churches.

To avoid discomfort, today's Pastors focus on GOD's Love. It is for the well-being of parishioners. But the Fear of GOD does not take long to stumble across in the Bible. GOD's Word mentions Fear of GOD from Genesis to Revelation. It does so in at least 144 Bible references. Nineteen of those are in the New Testament.

So, in the Bible, the fear of The LORD does not mean paralyzing terror or anxiety about GOD. It is not like fearing a dangerous person or situation. That would be a distraction from Satan. Instead, it shows a deep understanding of GOD's greatness. It also shows recognition of His power and His Divine nature. It is about acknowledging GOD's greatness and aligning oneself with His will.

Proverbs 9:10 states, "Respecting The LORD starts with wisdom. "Knowing the Holy One is understanding," the verse implies. Real wisdom comes from a deep respect for GOD. So, it is not about fear of punishment. It is also about understanding the importance of GOD's Character. It is about living by His Principles.

The Bible contains hundreds of stories. The writers highlight the fear of The LORD as a critical factor. It leads to wisdom, knowledge, and blessings. They often connect the phase to obedience. They connect it to righteousness and a desire to live by GOD's commandments.

We can always rely on GOD's Word as our defense because it will never fail us. GOD's Word is a refuge; it will never leave us during challenging seasons. Our faithfulness to His Word is the one place to hide from the enemy's attack.

THE fear of The LORD and love and trust are inseparable. It is a well-rounded approach, considering GOD's authority, grace, and mercy. The fear of The LORD is a crucial part of a believer's relationship with GOD.

Yet, the many spiritual distractions prevent us from developing. We must fight distractions. They are both tangible and intangible. We must fight them to hear from Jesus and grow closer to Jehovah. Again, the spiritual gifts aim to build up, encourage, and comfort the Church. Paul describes GOD as the "GOD of all comfort" (2 Corinthians 1:3).

Satan's primary aim is to create distractions, and he excels at it. He adores Christians who lose. The devil is indifferent to the means he employs to break our connection with the Holy Spirit. Each child of the King manifests the Spirit for the common good (1 Corinthians 12:7).

From a Christian view, Satan is a tempter and adversary. He seeks to lead people away from the Author and Perfecter of Our Faith. Satan's motivations in religious texts include rebelling against the Faithful and True Witnesses. He wanted to oppose and corrupt the creation of the Blessed and Only Ruler.

As Matthew 1:23 says, the enemy (Satan) is always scheming to take away Immanuel's children. He wants to remove and defeat them.

John Chapter Ten Verse Ten: "The thief comes only to steal, kill, and to destroy. I have come so they might have life and have it more." As Christians, we know that Satan only needs to divert our attention to win. And when he deters our attention, we lose contact with the Author and Perfecter of Our Faith (Hebrews 12:2).

Satan's natural inclination is to do whatever it takes to stop us from trusting Jesus as our LORD and Savior. His only option after losing that fight is to distract Christians. The vulnerability of Christians increases when they lack righteous focus. Thus, the devil has launched many strategies to keep every human distracted. In Christianity, believers must navigate many situations. These may lure them from their devotion.

When Christians believe they did wrong, they feel remorse. They seek reconciliation with their faith community through prayer or other

Sacred practices. Below are helpful ways to beat distractions and return to Jesus, the Alpha, and Omega (Revelation 1:8; 22:13).

a. TALK TO THE AUTHOR OF LIFE. YOU MUST COMMUNICATE TO BUILD A STRONG RELATIONSHIP WITH GOD, LIKE ANYONE ELSE.
b. GET INTO THE SCRIPTURES.
c. PAY CLOSE ATTENTION AND LISTEN CAREFULLY TO The LORD.
d. EXPRESS GRATITUDE: IT SHOWS JESUS WE APPRECIATE HIM.

However, isolation is one of the major causes of Christian distractions. When we isolate ourselves, we can expect to feel depressed. We become overly focused on ourselves. It can be a massive distraction for supporters of Jesus Christ.

When we find ourselves in solitude, we focus more on our thoughts and personal concerns. For a brief period, we focus on introspection. We stop caring about the affairs of others (Philippians 2:4). We grow distant from GOD and other believers. Detachment makes spiritual isolation an even more significant threat. Our inner quiet chatter disrupts our mental well-being. It affects our mood, thoughts, and actions.

But being alone can sometimes have its benefits. Despite that, connecting with others is crucial for your happiness and comfort. Still, balancing socializing and personal time is also beneficial. By being alone, you can think about your feelings, thoughts, dreams, problems, and past.

Time alone offers a rare chance to find and understand one's true self. It is beneficial. As you become more self-aware, you are more prone to do activities you enjoy. You will pursue captivating interests and be with people who uplift you.

Studies reveal a downside. Loneliness and isolation can cause health problems. These include heart disease, depression, and cognitive decline. We should examine Proverbs 18:1 more. It can help us avoid the cons of isolation and understand its causes and prevention.

For example, the writer of Proverbs explains this. When people isolate themselves, they seek their desires and rage against wise judgment. So, he advises against being or isolating oneself. He says selfishness and introversion drive inappropriate behavior. It implies that pursuing introverted interests hurts healthy relationships. And engaging in unnecessary conflicts goes against wise judgment. The verse encourages cultivating friendly relationships. It advises against isolating oneself or being divisive.

Isolation is a path to escapism. It helps people avoid the bad parts of life. These are those who have not faced life's challenges. They have turned to the world as an escape. They believe in Jesus, the Faithful and True Witness (Revelation 3:14). Still, this can block personal growth. It hinders the development of critical thinking skills. Relying on humans alone may hinder personal growth. It also blocks the development of critical thinking skills.

People turn to Christianity for distinct reasons. Their experiences and motivations can differ. For instance, some people may seek Holiness for short-term comfort during challenging times. So, it is incorrect to assume that all people choose righteousness to serve Jesus.

However, Christianity provides a framework for moral guidance. It also gives ethics guidance. It provides a sense of community and strength for everyone during tough times. People came to our Local Church for many reasons. But we must not let them distract us. The LORD has called us. The Saint's mission is to love GOD and others. They must share the pure Gospel, make disciples, live in Holiness and purity, and serve others.

The Apostle Paul writes, "My beloved brothers, be steadfast and immovable. Always abound in The LORD's work. Know that in The LORD your labor is not in vain" (1 Corinthians 15:58).

Finally, Satan is mischievous. He has even set up many preachers, Churches, and ministries. His goal is to deceive Christians and feed them lies that lead them away from the truth. Unfortunately, many Christians have fallen victim. They are now questioning their faith in GOD. Today, Lucifer has influencers on the internet who spread misleading information. They publish misinterpretations of the Holy Bible. The goal is to distract Christians from the valid Words of GOD.

Besides, the challenge of staying focused has plagued humanity since the beginning. But the current time is distinct and unparalleled. Experts are discussing the adverse effects. Hundreds of believers find it hard to focus and read the Holy Writ. Unable to concentrate because of constant thought interruption and reduced interest. Our focus on prayer and meditation is decreasing because we get distracted. The LORD's Prayer in Matthew 6:13 warns supporters of spiritual peril that needs GOD's help.

We create a dangerous distraction when we focus on unholiness over Holiness. Christians find it hard to focus on GOD. He gets sidetracked by trivial matters. The Bible calls this idolatry. When we focus on values, we deem them to be imperative. We may reveal our genuine passions when we get sidetracked.

Our unrighteous thoughts interrupt righteous fundamentals. We get distracted by unimportant things. But this distracts us from The Father. Our distractibility stems from our selfish nature at the deepest level.

It is hard to tell how many harmful factors are to blame. They cause our inattention despite this. But, if we ask GOD, He will free us from evil, no matter the cause. He will do this by using these powerful thoughts for our benefit. Pleasant thoughts help us find our desires. They also motivate us to be more sustainable by thinking. Philippians 4:6-8.

"Do not worry about anything. But, in every situation, pray to GOD. Ask with thanks. The peace of GOD surpasses all understanding. It will guard your hearts and minds in Christ Jesus. Finally, brothers and sisters, think about true things. They should also be noble, right, pure, lovely, and admirable. If something is excellent or praiseworthy, think about it."

Printed in the USA
CPSIA information can be obtained
at www.ICGtesting.com
CBHW021811050724
11152CB00001B/6